Whoa! Wait A Minute. What Was He Thinking Of?

Jake didn't have any intention of getting involved with anyone—not even Rebecca. Especially not 'Becca.

He'd been hired to do a job here, then he was going back to the mountains where he belonged. What Rebecca chose to do with her life was up to her.

"Jake? What is it? Why are you looking at me like that?"

"Like what?" he murmured, stroking her cheek with his finger.

"I don't know. As though you can't decide whether or not you want to kiss me again."

"Oh, there's no question that I want to kiss you again. The battle is whether I dare."

Dear Reader,

As always, I am proud to be bringing you the very best that romance has to offer—starting with an absolutely wonderful *Man of the Month* from Annette Broadrick called *Mysterious Mountain Man*. A book from Annette is always a real treat, and I know this story—her fortieth for Silhouette—will satisfy her fans and gain her new ones!

As readers, you've told me that you *love* miniseries, and you'll find some of the best series right here at Silhouette Desire. This month we have *The Cop and the Chorus Girl,* the second book in Nancy Martin's delightful *Opposites Attract* series, and *Dream Wedding,* the next book in Pamela Macaluso's *Just Married* series.

For those who like a touch of the supernatural, look for Linda Turner's *Heaven Can't Wait.* Lass Small's many fans will be excited about her latest, *Impulse.* And Kelly Jamison brings us a tender tale about a woman who returns to her hometown to confront her child's father in *Forsaken Father.*

Don't miss any of these great love stories!

Lucia Macro,
Senior Editor

Please address questions and book requests to:
Silhouette Reader Service
U.S.: 3010 Walden Ave., P.O. Box 1325, Buffalo, NY 14269
Canadian: P.O. Box 609, Fort Erie, Ont. L2A 5X3

Annette Broadrick

MYSTERIOUS MOUNTAIN MAN

SILHOUETTE *Desire*®
Published by Silhouette Books
America's Publisher of Contemporary Romance

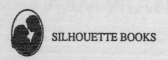 SILHOUETTE BOOKS

ISBN 0-373-05925-6

MYSTERIOUS MOUNTAIN MAN

Copyright © 1995 by Annette Broadrick

just inside the sagging screen door. "Thought I saw something movin' out there."

"You're dreamin', sweetheart. There's nothin' movin' around this part of West Texas 'cept maybe rattlesnakes and roadrunners."

Betty couldn't argue with him there. They were lucky to have a half-dozen customers a day during the winter months, mostly truckers passing through. An occasional motorist would stop for gas and might decide to eat, too.

The isolation never bothered her, because she was used to it. Both she and Mel had been born in the shadow of those mountains and most likely would die there, as well, which suited her just fine.

The moving cloud continued to grow larger until she recognized the spiraling tail of dust to be a vehicle driven at a high rate of speed over one of the area's dirt roads.

Identifying the sight only whetted her curiosity. The only road in that direction led directly into the mountains. It was too early in the year for the ranger station to be opened. No one else was around those parts, except for—

She chuckled.

"Now what?"

She turned away from the screen door and with quickened steps that belied both age and weight, moved behind the counter once more.

"Looks like Jake's decided to pay us a visit," she said, tossing out the half pot of coffee that had been sitting for several hours on the burner. She began to make a new pot.

One

Betty Abbott paused in her efforts to polish the counter of the Dry Gulch Café. She leaned forward and narrowed her eyes, attempting to pierce the grime-coated window of the eating establishment. Something was moving out there, which was unusual in the desolate terrain that surrounded the small settlement. After concentrating for several moments, she made out a tiny swirl of dust at the foot of the Guadalupe Mountains.

Dropping the rag, she moved from behind the counter to get a better look.

"Whatcha lookin' at?"

She glanced toward the serving window of the kitchen at Mel, her husband of forty-two years, before peering back outside. "I'm not sure." She paused

ANNETTE BROADRICK

believes in romance and the magic of life. Since 1984, when her first book was published, Annette has shared her view of life and love with readers all over the world. In addition to being nominated by *Romantic Times* as one of the Best New Authors of that year, she has also won the *Romantic Times* Reviewers' Choice Award for Best in its Series for *Heat of the Night, Mystery Lover* and *Irresistible;* the *Romantic Times* WISH Award for her heroes in *Strange Enchantment, Marriage Texas Style!* and *Impromptu Bride;* and *Romantic Times'* Lifetime Achievement Awards for Series Romance and Series Romantic Fantasy.

"Can't be Jake, honey. He was just here a few weeks ago."

"I don't care if he was here yestiddy. There's nobody around here that drives like a bat outta hell the way Jake does. You just wait 'n' see if that ain't him."

Mel pushed open the swinging door between the kitchen and the eating area and walked through. "You really think it's him, huh?" He squinted through the window made opaque by the never-ending West Texas dust storms.

Betty didn't look up from her task of pouring water into the coffeemaker. "Ya wanna bet?"

Mel shook his head. "Hell, no, woman. If I paid off all the bets you've won from me over the years, you'd be a rich woman."

She paused long enough to flash him a saucy smile, holding the premeasured packet of coffee in one hand, a thin white filter in the other. "Keep your money, honey. I'm already rich with everything that really counts in life."

Mel slipped his arm around her ample waist and hugged her. "That makes two of us."

She finished the coffee preparations before turning in his arms and giving him a quick squeeze in return. "D'ya got any cinnamon rolls left? You know how Jake loves them things."

"If it *is* Jake, then I'm gonna have to compliment him on his sensitive nose. I made a fresh batch this morning that should be coming out of the oven anytime now."

Mel headed back to the kitchen, and Betty took up her vigil once more at the door of the café.

The dust cloud steadily increased in size until she could see the vehicle causing it. A battered pickup truck of some undetermined color moved across the horizon, growing larger in her view.

Yep, that's Jake, she decided with an absent nod. *I wonder what he's doing back so soon?* Who could ever figure out Jake Taggart? He was a law unto himself.

Betty remembered the night he was born. How could she forget? His mother, Mary Whitefeather Taggart, would always live in Betty's memories as a sweet, gentle woman who'd never deserved the hard licks life had given her. She'd been abandoned by that no-account Johnny Taggart six months after he'd sweet-talked her into marrying him, pretending he wanted to settle down.

She'd believed him, fool that she was. He'd left her stranded in West Texas, pregnant and alone.

Betty and Mel had insisted she stay there with them, while she had insisted on working for her room and board. A person couldn't help loving the quiet woman with the desolate black eyes, who hadn't wanted to be any trouble to anybody.

She hadn't told them she was in labor until too late to get her some medical attention. Betty'd had to help with the birthing. She and Mel had lost their only baby two years before, even though she'd gone to the hospital in El Paso. This time, Betty had vowed that she would help this new life into the world if God would show her what to do.

She would never forget those long hours, or Mel's supportive presence in the background—his calm assurance that his wife could do anything she set her mind to, including deliver a baby out in the middle of nowhere.

Betty knew that God had kept His promise; otherwise, where would she have found the strength to have done all the necessary things to coax the angry young Jake into presenting himself? He'd entered the world with an attitude, bless his heart, with clenched fists and a strong will to beat the odds against him.

She couldn't love him more than if he'd come from her own womb.

Betty watched the distant truck careen onto the highway without slowing down. The dust cloud began to dissipate now that there was nothing to fuel it. The truck moved rapidly toward them.

"Yep," Mel muttered. "You were right."

Why is Jake coming down from his place in the mountains so soon after his last visit? she wondered.

She glanced at the coffee to make sure it would be ready when he arrived, then turned back and watched Jake's progress along the highway.

Jake drove like he did everything else he ever put his mind to—with a skill and careless elegance that drew the eye. Easily in command of the machine he drove, Jake pulled into the graveled parking area and slowed to a stop in the empty lot.

Betty stood in the doorway and watched as he opened the truck door and unfolded his long length. He pulled his battered Stetson low over his forehead so that it touched the rim of his aviator sunglasses. He wore a sheepskin-lined denim jacket that fit snugly across his broad shoulders, then tapered to his lean waist. When he reached back into the truck for his keys, his tight jeans revealed the long, muscular legs and taut buttocks of a runner. Well-worn hiking boots covered his feet as he sauntered across the parking lot toward the café.

Not for the first time Betty thought about the number of women who'd wanted to lasso and tie down the man walking toward her. Despite her age, she could understand very well their reaction to him. He seemed to bristle with energy even when his movements appeared slow and measured. There was an aliveness about him that caught the eye. He was a fine specimen of the human male animal in the prime of life.

She admired him as much as she loved him. He'd accepted the cards life had dealt him and had played them with a fierceness and determination that had never folded regardless of the stakes. And yet, there was something about him that remained a mystery. Jake Taggart was a very private man. She'd learned years ago not to question him about his decisions and choices, even when she didn't understand them. Jake never let anyone get too close to him.

Betty waited until she saw his rare smile flash like a brilliant light in his sun-darkened face before she spoke.

"What happened? Did you forget somethin' when you were down here last time?"

Jake stepped up onto the slanted porch that ran the length of the building. She pushed the door open for him and he took it with one hand while he pulled off his sunshades with the other. His black eyes danced with mischief.

"I couldn't handle another day without seeing you, sweetheart. You're downright irresistible and you know it."

"I heard that," Mel yelled from the kitchen. "You'd better watch how you flirt with my wife, fella. If you ain't careful, I'll have ta take ya behind the buildin' and whup some sense inta ya."

Jake's smile flashed once more. "You and what army, pal?"

Their familiar ritual of greeting complete, the three people burst into laughter while Jake gave Betty a hug that lifted her off her feet and made her squeal. Once he released her she went over to pour him a cup of fresh coffee.

Jake pulled off his Stetson and sank down on one of the stools alongside the counter. Betty filled a thick ceramic mug with steaming liquid and set it in front of him. Mel came out of the kitchen and put a cinnamon roll, glistening with fresh glaze, in front of Jake.

Jake glanced around the small café that had been a part of his childhood, as though seeing it for the first time. He became conscious of the scarred tables and chairs, the linoleum whose design had been scrubbed and wiped off years ago and the worn countertop.

A couple of oil paintings hung on the back wall, mute evidence that Betty and Mel would never turn away anyone who was hungry, even if the person was broke. Those two scenes of El Capitan—the majestic peak of the Guadalupe range—and the surrounding desert area were their payment for feeding a fellow who had camped out for a few weeks in the vicinity many years ago.

"So what are you doin' here?" Betty asked once again.

Jake pretended dismay. "You mean I've already worn out my welcome for the winter?" He took a huge bite of the roll and almost groaned out loud from the savory sensation.

She punched his arm. "You know better 'n that. But you came down here for supplies just a while ago. We didn't expect to see you again anytime soon."

He took a sip of coffee, giving himself time to think about his answer. "I guess the truth is that I'm getting a little bored with my own company these days."

Mel called from the kitchen. "Betty, don't forget to give him the card that fella left here a couple of weeks ago."

"Oh, yeah. Good thing you reminded me. I'd done forgot all about that." Betty walked over to the old-fashioned cash register and slid her fingers beneath it, coming out with a card. "Here you go. This guy showed up and was asking all kinds of questions about you... like where you lived and if you had a telephone or a fax or something. I told him that nobody knew where exactly you lived up in them mountains, not even the park rangers."

She smiled when she said that, to remind Jake that she knew of his unauthorized use of land that had been claimed by the government as a national park area several years after he'd made his home there.

When he continued to eat the sweet roll without changing expression, she added, "He asked us to give you his card the next time we saw you."

Jake took the card and immediately recognized the logo in the corner. The address was familiar as well. CPI Enterprises in Seattle, Washington. The name meant nothing to him; he'd never heard of a Woodrow Forrester. He must have been hired after Jake left the company. He placed the card on the counter and sipped his coffee without comment.

She waited for a few minutes, then said, "He insisted it was real important for him to get in touch with you as soon as possible. Like it was some kind of an emergency or something."

Jake took another bite of the roll.

"Isn't that the company where you used to work?"

He finished chewing and took a sip of coffee before replying. "That was a long time ago."

She looked at him, puzzled. "Not so long, surely. You've been back about a year, haven't you?"

"Thirteen months."

She nodded her head in agreement. "That ain't so long a time, when you think about it. You worked for that company how long?"

"Almost five years . . . but that's all ancient history now."

She lifted one eyebrow and tapped the card with a pudgy forefinger. "Well, young man, I'd say your history's tryin' to catch up with you."

He stuck the card in his shirt pocket. "Only if I let it." He took another bite of the savory roll. He'd never found a pastry anywhere to compare with Mel's cinnamon rolls. They were worth the long trek out of the mountains.

He glanced up and realized that Betty was still standing on the other side of the counter, watching him. As soon as she made eye contact with him, she spoke.

"Whadduya s'pose this guy wants?"

"Who knows?" He wished she'd drop the subject, but he knew Betty too well to think she would.

"So. You goin' to call 'im?"

That took no conscious thought at all. "Nope."

She crossed her arms and leaned her hip against the counter. "Just out of orneryness, I s'pose?"

Jake straightened, fighting to control his impatience. Betty knew nothing about his reasons for leaving the company. Only Brock Adams, the head of the company, knew. Once Jake left, he'd never discussed the matter with anyone.

Whoever this Forrester character represented in the company, Jake knew it wouldn't be Brock Adams.

Betty was still eyeing him expectantly. "Look, Betty. It would be a waste of time for me to call this guy. I have nothing to say to him or anybody else in that company. I'm no longer a part of that world." He glanced out the window and nodded toward the mountains. "That's my life now. I've returned to my roots."

"You know, Jake," Betty said. "I suppose most people would probably believe ya, but I happen to remember how hard you worked all them years to get your education. I was there, remember? You took all kinds of part-time jobs, refusing to let me and Mel help ya, no matter how hard you had to struggle. You even got yourself some sports scholarships by playing your heart out, all so you could get the kind of education you needed to make it in the business world. I'm afraid you ain't going to convince me that all that effort you went to meant nothing to you. I don't care what you say."

He supposed she had a point. Maybe he needed to look at things from a different perspective now that he'd had some time to himself. CPI Enterprises wasn't the only company in the world, even if he'd spent his years there being groomed to succeed Brock Adams, thinking the company would be his life.

At the time he'd left, all he'd wanted was to leave the business world behind. He'd returned to the Guadalupes in search of some kind of inner peace, a way to live with the choices he'd made.

He'd ignored the park rangers and their petty governmental rules that said he could no longer have a home in the national park area. He'd actually made a game of circumventing them while he turned the shack he'd built up there as a kid into a habitable home.

Eventually he'd formed an uneasy but peaceful coexistence with them. He ignored them and they left him alone.

The months of hard physical labor had done him good. He'd come to terms with his life. He'd accepted the kinds of behavior he could live with and had set boundaries for those he couldn't. The mountains had done their healing work on him. Maybe it was time for him to look at his options and consider what he wanted to do next.

One option he knew he'd never consider would be to return to Seattle and the life he'd once attempted to establish there.

Mel came out of the kitchen and poured himself a cup of coffee. He studied Jake for a moment before he asked, "How 'bout a game of dominoes?"

Jake nodded. "Sounds good." He picked up his cup, stepped behind the counter for a refill, then followed Mel over to one of the tables in the back. He set the cup down and pulled off his coat, hanging it on a nearby hook before he sat down across from the older man.

Mel and Betty were the closest thing he had to family. He loved them with a deep-seated sense of loyalty and appreciation. But he still couldn't talk to them about his life and the choices he'd made. He knew that they loved and accepted him, but they had trouble understanding him.

He wasn't any good at trying to talk about his feelings. He never had been. He'd learned early on that if he was going to survive, he had to depend on himself. Nobody else. He'd never been one to talk about himself, about his goals in life. About his dreams.

After his mother had died, he'd been like a half-wild animal, snarling at everybody, resisting any authority. He hadn't trusted many people in his life, that's for sure. Mel and Betty, of course. Hell. They'd more than half raised him.

And Brock Adams. For whatever reason, he'd learned to trust and admire Brock Adams during the years they'd worked so closely together. He'd made an error in judgment, though, believing in Brock, believing he knew the kind of man Brock was. And he'd paid for the error. He'd left a well-paid job and a promising career without looking back or regretting the cost.

Payment enough in any man's book.

So why in hell were they looking for him now, after all this time?

"You gonna play or just sit starin' at the spots?" Mel asked, breaking into Jake's thoughts.

Jake blinked, suddenly focusing on the dominoes in front of him for the first time in several minutes. "Sorry, guess my mind was wandering."

"No need to be sorry. This ain't brain surgery. You're allowed to take all the time you want, but I'm going to have to get to work here directly," Mel responded, glancing at the clock over the front door.

Jake studied the layout before him, then placed a domino along one line.

"Maybe I shoulda kept my mouth shut. Looks like you're gonna beat me if I don't do somethin' mighty fast here."

Jake scratched his chin. He hadn't shaved in a couple of days, another sign of his abstraction. He'd been taking long hikes lately, now that he'd finished all the construction plans for his place. Sometimes he would end up camping out overnight if he was too far from the cabin when the winter dusk caught up with him.

"Gettin' restless up there in them mountains, aren't you?"

"A little," Jake admitted.

"I could never figure out why you wanted to live up there all alone, anyway."

Jake grinned. "I'm far from alone, Mel. There's plenty of company. Most of the time I much prefer Mother Nature and her wildlife to people. At least the predators are easier to recognize."

"Don't you ever miss that job you had out in Seattle?"

Jake frowned. "Sometimes."

"I can't rightly remember what it was they made at that factory."

"They manufactured various parts used in the building of airplanes, helicopters—whatever the aeronautical industry needed."

"Do you suppose that guy that was here is wanting to offer you a job?"

"Wouldn't matter if he was."

Neither one of them spoke for a while. One game ended and they started another without a word. Occasionally Betty came over and refilled their coffee cups.

"You guys gettin' hungry?" Betty finally asked.

Mel grunted. Jake glanced up. "I could probably eat a sandwich."

The sound of tires on the gravel driveway outside announced that the tiny restaurant would soon have more business. Jake leaned back in his chair and watched a couple with two small children get out of a late-model minivan.

"Looks like your noon rush just arrived," he drawled, grinning. Mel hurried to the kitchen while Betty reached for the stack of menus, a smile on her face for the children.

* * *

Rebecca Adams had been following the arrow-straight highway east out of El Paso for what seemed like hours, looking for the Dry Gulch Café. The desolate West Texas terrain had so mesmerized her with its sameness that she almost drove past the small settlement without noticing it. She was almost upon it before she noticed the sign advertising the café.

She peered at the cluster of weathered, gray buildings while hurriedly braking to make the turn. There were only two vehicles in the gravel parking lot—a minivan and a pickup truck.

Rebecca quickly glanced into the rearview mirror of her rental car, thankful there was no one to see that she hadn't bothered to signal her intentions as she pulled off the highway. She parked neatly beside the angled truck and turned off the car engine.

She'd left Seattle early that morning and hadn't paused in her travels since. Woody had told her that the only people he'd found who seemed to know anything about Jake Taggart were here at this café.

She took a deep breath and slowly released it. She was here now, ready to begin her search for the elusive Mr. Taggart. She'd made up her mind that nothing was going to stop her from finding Jake and talking to him, no matter what she had to do.

She quickly ran a comb through her dark, shoulder-length hair, powdered her nose and checked to make sure she still had on her lipstick. Her wide-set gray eyes stared back at her apprehensively from her compact mirror. She couldn't remember when she'd ever been so nervous before, but then she'd never had to deal with such high stakes before. She couldn't afford to lose this particular gamble.

She could think of any number of people she would have preferred to look for besides Jake Taggart. She'd never understood her father's enthusiasm about the man. He may have been a genius at what he did for the company, but he'd been an impossible person to get to know.

She'd always taken pride in the fact that she could figure most people out. She'd made human behavior her main study, but Jake had always managed to elude her analysis.

As soon as she stepped out of the car, Rebecca paused to straighten her slim dark skirt and adjust the tailored matching jacket that stopped a few inches above the mid-thigh length of her skirt. She reached for her briefcase, which held her purse, and straightened, inwardly seeking the professional calm that carried her through her daily working routine.

The gravel made walking in heels difficult. She picked her way carefully across the dusty expanse. The last thing she needed was an injury of some sort out here in this godforsaken wilderness.

She was relieved to reach the smoother surface of the picturesque porch, which held a cluster of chairs—straight-backed and rockers—and a couple of tables. She glanced around her, perplexed by the evidence of her own eyes. Had Jake Taggart actually grown up in this area? In no way did it fit the image of the man she remembered.

The sagging screen door protested with a squeal when she pushed it open and stepped inside.

Her appearance seemed to have frozen the few occupants in the room into suspended animation. Every eye seemed to be trained on her. A casually dressed man and woman occupied a nearby booth with two small children. The little girl sat in a high chair at the end of the table, while the boy was perched on a booster seat beside his father.

All four stared at her as though she'd just stepped off a space ship and was there to make inquiries of the local inhabitants.

The woman behind the counter stood with a forgotten coffeepot in her hand, her eyes round as she stared at the newcomer.

Only the cowboy in the back seemed uninterested in her. He sat with his chair leaning against the wall, balanced on two legs, as though he had nothing better to do than to hang around a café all day. His thick black hair was worn too long, brushing his collar and tumbling across his forehead. He'd glanced at her when she'd first walked in, then he'd looked away as though unimpressed, while casually twirling a pair of sunglasses by one of the earpieces.

Rebecca gripped her briefcase tighter and approached the woman behind the counter.

"Good afternoon, miss," the woman said before Rebecca could speak. "Are you here for lunch?"

Intent on her mission, Rebecca paused, feeling a little off-balance. For the first time in several hours she realized she hadn't eaten since she'd left home. She took in the room in another sweeping glance before replying.

"I—uh—yes, actually, that would be nice."

She was a little irritated with herself for not thinking about eating here. The woman must think her ridiculous to appear surprised to be offered a meal in a café. What, after all, had she expected? She certainly hadn't walked into a lending library!

Rebecca noticed an empty booth in the back and had started toward it before she realized that she would be sitting near the cowboy. She certainly hoped he didn't think she was trying to get his attention!

Taking another firm grip on her briefcase, she straightened her shoulders slightly and continued toward the back of the room without looking at anyone.

"Hello, Rebecca," a deep voice drawled from somewhere close by.

She spun around, almost losing her balance. How could anyone here know who she—? Only one person could possibly recognize her. Her gaze darted around the room before she made eye contact with the cowboy, who continued to watch her without moving from his comfortable, laid-back position.

For the first time since she'd entered the café Rebecca really looked at the man leaning his chair against the wall.

"Jake," she whispered almost to herself as she stared at him. Her breath seemed caught in her throat. Whatever her expectations had been for this trip, finding Jake within moments after her arrival had never crossed her mind.

He took his time looking at her, allowing his gaze to wander from the top of her head, lingering over the trim-fitting suit, before pausing on her now dusty pumps.

Eventually his gaze met her eyes. "What brings you to these parts?" he drawled. "Did you make a wrong turn somewhere?"

In the year since she'd last seen him, Rebecca had forgotten how his low voice had always caused her spine to tingle in a most unexpected and unprofessional way. The tingle was back, darn it, and they'd barely exchanged any words. She stood taller in an effort to combat her unwanted reaction to the man.

The waitress spoke from directly behind her. "You can sit anywhere, miss. Just pick a spot and light."

Rebecca glanced around at the waitress just as she heard the other two legs on Jake's chair hit the floor.

"She'll take the back booth, Betty," he said, straightening in slow motion to his full height. "Bring her Mel's special. Let's show the city lady what down-home cookin's all about."

Gently he touched Rebecca's arm and guided her over to the booth. He didn't take his eyes off her as she numbly slid onto the bench seat, staring at him as he sat down across from her.

This long-haired, unshaven cowboy was Jake Taggart? She could scarcely believe the evidence of her own eyes. What had happened to the man in the business suits and ties with the professionally styled hair and freshly laundered shirts?

Nothing about this meeting was going as she had planned. She hadn't tried to guess how she'd find him or where a meeting between them would take place but this unexpected encounter had left her reeling. All of the remarks she'd carefully planned to say to him had left her mind.

While she was frantically searching for a light remark, Jake said, "Betty, I'd like you to meet Rebecca Adams. She works for CPI Enterprises in Seattle." He glanced at Rebecca out of the corner of his eye before adding, "Besides being the head of the personnel department, she's the boss's daughter."

He glanced back at her, no doubt waiting for her reaction to his remark. Since he wasn't the first person through the years to imply that she held a responsible position in the company only because of her father, she chose not to comment.

She really didn't care what Jake Taggart thought of her. She knew she was good at her job. She didn't owe anyone any explanations or apologies for the position she held.

When she remained silent, he continued. "Betty and Mel own the restaurant. They serve the best food west of the Mississippi."

Rebecca noticed the older woman—Betty had he called her?— blushed like a schoolgirl. But then, Jake seemed to have that effect on most women—even her, darn him—despite her determination to keep a professional distance between them. How could she have forgotten this man's charisma? Hadn't she once accused her father of being unduly influenced by Jake's magnetism as well as his professional expertise?

"Pleased ta meet cha, Ms. Adams. What would you like to drink?"

"I think I'll have—"

"They don't have any of your herbal teas, 'Becca, and the coffee is chock-full of caffeine," Jake drawled, deliberately baiting her.

Ignoring him, she smiled at Betty and said, "Coffee sounds wonderful. Thank you."

Betty hurried away, presumably for a cup since she was still holding the pot of coffee in her hand. Jake, meanwhile, turned sideways in the booth—his back resting against the wall, his elbow on the table, and his long legs stretched along the length of the bench seat.

Rebecca folded her hands together on the table and studied them in an effort to organize her thoughts.

"You never said what brings you to these parts, 'Becca." The slight tilt of his mouth revealed his awareness of her efforts at control.

She lifted her gaze to meet his. Thankfully, to her, her voice sounded steady when she replied, "That should be obvious, Jake. I came looking for you."

Two

Jake studied her for a long moment. She couldn't tell what he was thinking, but then, she never could. This man continued to be an enigma to her. Despite her working knowledge of human nature, she'd never been able to figure out what made Jake Taggart tick.

She knew she was at a disadvantage with him and that she would have to call on everything she had to convince him to do what she so desperately needed him to do. She'd come this far. She couldn't blow it now.

She took a deep breath, prepared to make her pitch, when he said, "I'm downright flattered, 'Becca." There wasn't an ounce of sincerity in his voice. "I'll admit to being surprised to see you here."

Now *that* she could believe despite the fact that he'd concealed his surprise well. She looked toward the dusty windows and beyond to the brightly lit sky. "West Texas is certainly different from Seattle, I must admit." She turned back to face the man across from her. She'd always found him formidable. "Did anyone tell you that we've been trying to contact you?"

He opened his mouth as though to answer her, then paused, glancing past her shoulder. Betty arrived with a cup of coffee. She set it in front of Rebecca before turning to Jake. "You want some more coffee?"

"No, thanks. Water's fine."

Betty smiled at Rebecca, her eyes reflecting her curiosity. "So you came to see Jake, did ya?" she asked, making no attempt to hide her interest.

Rebecca was surprised. She wasn't used to having a server make personal conversation. "I—uh—" She stopped, not knowing how to respond. She was out of her element and wasn't certain what was called for here, according to proper etiquette.

"It's all right," Betty said, her voice filled with sympathetic understanding. "He's used to women chasing after him." She turned to Jake. "So. You expectin' to hang around here overnight, or do you intend to git back home?"

Jake lazily stretched before replying. "Haven't decided yet, Betty."

"Well, we always keep your room ready for ya," she said casually, before returning to the cash register where the other diners were waiting to pay for their meal.

Rebecca knew it was none of her business, but she asked, anyway. "Are you related to Betty?"

"In a manner of speaking."

She nodded, more to herself than anything. "I wondered about that when I saw them listed in your personnel file. It was our only lead to your whereabouts."

After straightening the knife, fork and spoon that Betty had placed in front of him, Jake picked up the spoon with his thumb and forefinger and began to flip it, tapping one end on the table, flipping it, then tapping the other end, as though he had nothing better to do than to make a repetitive noise no doubt designed to irritate her. She glanced at his long fingers, then away.

"Well, now you've found me. So what do you want?"

She took a sip of the coffee, her mind racing with questions and comments. She mentally replayed what Betty had said just now and surprised herself by verbalizing the least important question flitting through her mind.

"Is that true?" she asked.

"Is what true?"

"Are you used to women chasing after you?"

He twitched his shoulders and gave a quick shake of his head. "That was Betty's way of pulling my leg."

She dropped her gaze to the steaming liquid. She was stalling and she knew it, but she couldn't seem to bring any order to her thoughts at the moment. To immediately find the man for whom she'd been prepared to make a diligent search had thrown her off her stride. She needed a moment to regroup and to marshal all her arguments.

"What do you want, Rebecca?" he repeated, impatiently. "Did Brock send you?"

She stiffened for a moment before answering him. "No."

"I didn't think so." Tension filled the silence between them before he continued, his tone mocking. "As I recall, you never went out of your way to spend much time in my company when I worked at CPI, so it's hard for me to guess what prompted this little visit."

Rebecca lowered her cup, carefully replacing it on the table. He certainly wasn't making this meeting an easy one. What, after all, had she expected? Before she could comment on his remark, he continued by saying, "You think I never noticed how studiously you managed to avoid me?" His mouth curled slightly. "I was aware I wasn't your idea of a corporate executive. Well, don't worry. After a few years I came to the same conclusion, myself. Guess I don't have the necessary killer instinct."

She controlled her surprise at this unexpected glimpse into the way his mind worked. "On the contrary, Jake. I thought you were an excellent executive. Since my father planned for you to take his place in the company, his views were obvious, as well." She paused, searching for an explanation of something she'd never before attempted to put into words. "As for me, I'll admit that I never went out of my way to get to know you, that's true." She forced herself to meet his dark-eyed gaze before saying, "I'm not particularly proud of the fact, but the truth is, for some time I was jealous of you.''

His eyes narrowed and he quirked one of his eyebrows at her, but he made no comment.

She shrugged. ''Hopefully I've gotten over that rather adolescent reaction to the fact that my dad treated you like the son he never had.''

''And that bothered you?''

''It shouldn't have, of course. There was no rational reason for me to see you as a threat. I never had any interest in learning to run the company. I much prefer working with the employees and leaving the rest of the business to the engineering and business majors. I never made any secret of my professional preferences.''

''But you aren't talking about professional preferences now, are you?''

This wasn't the topic she'd intended to discuss with him. Somehow, she'd lost control of their meeting before she'd had an opportunity to state her reasons for being there. He'd gotten a reaction from her. He was good at that—causing a reaction without giving anything of himself away.

She sighed and shook her head. ''I've had the past year to look at my behavior, to recognize and face how childish I was acting by distancing myself from you.'' She glanced away before forcing herself to meet his gaze. ''However, you have to admit you're not an easy man to get to know, even in the best of circumstances.''

''I had a job to do. I was never out to win any popularity contests . . . with you or anybody else.''

She couldn't resist a quick look at the way he was dressed. He still wasn't attempting to impress anyone. Not that it mattered to her what he looked like or how he treated her. However, it would make her mission much easier if they could find a common ground.

She needed his help, yet she resented having to ask for it. There'd been so many upheavals in her life lately, so much over which she had no control. She hated to ask anyone for anything. She'd grown up independent and self-reliant, traits her father admired, traits she'd continued to foster as she grew from the idolizing child to the adult who better understood her own motives.

Her studies of human behavior and her degrees in psychology had helped her to deal with many of those unresolved childhood issues. What they hadn't taught her was how to deal with an attractive man whose dark gaze managed to affect her pulse rate despite her understanding of chemical attraction and the theory behind opposites attracting. She didn't want to be attracted to this man. She wanted her interest in him to be strictly a professional one.

"I never understood why you left CPI," she said, hoping to prod him into explaining more about who he was and what made him tick. Knowing his motives might also assist her in finding the most positive way to suggest he return to work for the company. "You were good at what you did. You had a bright future with the company."

He picked up his glass of water and took a drink from it. After he set the glass down, he murmured,

"My reasons for leaving don't really matter after all this time."

She straightened, placing her hands in her lap, hoping to downplay her nervousness. "Perhaps not," she said carefully. "I suppose the more pertinent question to ask you is, what can I offer you to get you to return to CPI?"

He made a chopping motion with his hand. "Is that what this is all about—what you're doing here? Do you think Brock is going to allow me to walk back into the company and take up my old position? You should have checked with him first before you came running to me with any offers. Brock Adams knows what I think of the policies and procedures in that company. He knows exactly why I left and why I won't go back."

"My father is dead, Jake."

Her words hung between them as though taking on a life of their own, crowding the small space with sudden emotion.

Jake slowly straightened his slouching position. "Dead?" he repeated. "Brock?" His voice roughened. "When? What happened?"

She bit her lip in an effort to remain composed. Talking about her father's death was still difficult. "Six months ago." She paused and took a sip of water. "He died in his sleep. The doctor said it was his heart."

Jake swung his legs off the seat and turned so that he was facing her. His face had been washed clean of expression. He stared at her blankly, his eyes unreadable.

"Was there any warning?"

"If there was, he never mentioned it. He began working longer hours after you left, rarely getting home before midnight. I tried to talk to him, tried to get him to rest, but he ignored me." Her voice hardened. "If you hadn't left the company, he might be alive today."

Her words were as effective as a slap in the face...or a fist to his gut. Brock was dead. Only now, now that he'd learned that Brock was dead did he realize how he had viewed Brock Adams—as an Olympian figure, an immortal god who could not concern himself with the problems of mere mortals. Concerns about ethics and conscience and accountability hadn't been as important as other considerations—growth, and returns, and happy stockholders.

Jake had been so angry when he'd left...angry, disgusted and frustrated. He hadn't cared to listen to more of Brock's explanations and rationalizations for his decisions. Jake had had enough.

Now Brock was dead and it was obvious from Rebecca's determined efforts to contact him that the situation had not gotten any better since he'd left.

Now she wanted him to return to CPI. The idea was laughable. However, Jake didn't feel much like laughing at the moment. After the shock of her news, he wasn't certain what he was feeling.

Betty's appearance with two platters of steaming food was a welcome respite from charged emotions.

The appetizing aroma caused Rebecca's stomach to growl in anticipation.

Jake glanced at the plate in front of him, reminded of his earlier order. "This is a sandwich?"

Betty placed her hands on her hips. "Mel decided you might be hungrier than you thought." She gave a sideways glance to Rebecca. "You've gotta keep up your strength, you know."

He just shook his head and picked up his fork, knowing there was no winning an argument against the Abbotts. He glanced across the table. Rebecca must have been hungry. She wasn't wasting any time on conversation, which was just as well. He needed some space to adjust to the information she'd given him.

He waited until she finished eating before he asked, "Who is running CPI these days?"

He watched her carefully blot her lips with the napkin. "As my father's sole heir, I inherited his controlling interest in the company. I took over as chairman of the board, but at the moment there is no managing director."

He remembered some of the sharks who were department heads and smiled. "I bet the place is experiencing a real feeding frenzy these days."

Betty came and removed their plates, refilled Rebecca's coffee cup and Jake's water glass and left before she responded. She leaned her crossed arms on the table. "I always thought I was fairly competent at reading and understanding people, until I had all this dumped into my lap. I freely concede that I'm in way over my head at the moment. I don't have the training, the ability or the personality to take over the helm and run the place, not the way you do. Obviously you can see why I'm here, why I wanted to talk to you, to explain what's happening."

"Ambition and greed aren't difficult to identify, 'Becca. You can find it in every business endeavor. Hell, it's part of the human experience."

"There's more going on, Jake. Since Dad died we've had what I believe to be acts of sabotage taking place in the plant—shipments delayed, bills of lading misplaced, equipment breaking down. Somebody's working hard to make us look bad. And it's having the desired effect."

"What do you think I could do about it?"

"My father had a great deal of confidence in you. He never told me why you left. In fact, he refused to discuss you with me at all, but I well remember how pleased he was earlier with the way you justified the decision he made to hire you. If you had a falling out with him then I think we need to look at the present picture without allowing the past to distort the situation. You are the only person who knows the business well enough to be able to step in and pull it through this crisis. The company needs you."

Jake didn't answer right away. Rebecca forced herself to remain quiet, hoping she'd said enough, hoping she hadn't said too much to turn him off the idea. She was convinced that Jake Taggart was the only person who could help save the company.

When he finally spoke, she was shaken by his response. "I want no part of that life," he said in a flat voice. "I'm content where I am."

Rebecca couldn't afford to accept his decision. She glanced around the room, which had fallen silent with the departure of the other diners. She could hear the couple who ran the place talking in the kitchen. Her gaze went to the grimy windows and, looking past them, to the desolate landscape.

In an effort to buy herself needed time to think of a different approach, she asked, "This is where you grew up?"

"That's right."

"It's rather isolated, isn't it?"

His small smile was lopsided. "Yep."

"What is there here for you to do?"

The fact that he'd been asking himself the same question during the past few days didn't endear her to him. "I don't need much to survive."

"My father used to say that you thrived on challenge."

He nodded toward the window. "There's challenge enough."

"Is there?" She tilted her head slightly and looked at him. "Physically, I suppose there is. But mentally? Emotionally? What kind of challenges are you finding here?"

"What is this? A new form of job interview?"

She nodded. "That's exactly what it is, Jake. CPI needs you and your talents. You must know that. Your leaving was a blow to the company as well as to my father, whether he ever admitted it or not. I don't think either one fully recovered from your absence. If you'd been there, none of this would have happened. The transition after my dad's death would have been orderly and without the turmoil we've been going through."

"No one's indispensable, 'Becca."

"True. But some positions are more easily filled than others."

He reached into his pocket and pulled out the card he'd placed there earlier. He gave a flip to his wrist, and the card landed between them. "Who's Woodrow Forrester?"

She didn't need to read the card. "He's in charge of accounting. Dad hired him not long after you left. He's the one who pointed out the urgency of the situation we're in. When I told him about you and what I felt you could do for us, he volunteered to come looking for you."

Jake drummed his fingers on the table. Then he ran his fingers through his hair. "It wouldn't work," he finally muttered.

"Why not?"

He just shook his head, refusing to say anything more.

Her chest ached and she realized that she'd been holding her breath. She forced herself to fill her lungs with much-needed air, praying for inspiration. She'd counted on the fact that once he knew how serious the situation was, he would be willing to return.

Regardless of her personal reaction to him, she knew that Jake Taggart was exactly what the company needed.

"Is it because of me? I mean, what you said earlier about my appearing uncomfortable around you? Is it that you don't want to work for me?"

"I've never given a thought about your opinion of me, one way or the other. As far as I was concerned, we both worked for the same company and had similar goals. We didn't have to like each other.''

She glanced down at her clasped hands. ''It isn't that I dislike you, Jake,'' she said slowly, searching for words that might make a difference to his decision. ''I used to feel— That is, there were times when I felt as though you could read my mind, as though I had no secrets where you were concerned.'' She gave a nervous chuckle. ''Let's face it. You can be rather intimidating at times.''

He didn't say anything right away. Instead, he waited until she looked up at him before he said quietly, ''You've got a very expressive face, 'Becca. It isn't difficult to tell what you're thinking most of the time.''

She kept her gaze steady. ''Then you must know how badly I need your help at the plant. I've tried these past few months to keep everything together. I've taken on more staff, mostly in personnel, to free me for other areas. I never wanted to be the one running things. My father understood that, which is why he trained you for the job. He'd intended to retire and—'' Her voice broke and she couldn't go on.

Jake looked around the small café, feeling uneasy about the turn in the conversation. He'd told her no, hadn't he? He'd told her that he was happy where he was, but was he being completely honest with himself? Hadn't CPI been his focus for several years?

Leaving the company had been one of the toughest things he'd ever done. He'd felt betrayed by Brock Adams and the choices the man had made despite Jake's warnings. Jake had expected more from Brock than that. Hell, he'd looked up to Brock, admired him, wanted to be just like him...until the day Jake realized that his own integrity was more important to him than his ambition.

Rebecca's voice broke into his thoughts. "I understand you live in those mountains." She nodded toward the windows.

"That's right."

"Is it difficult to get to your home?"

He shrugged. "Depends on how you define difficult. You can't drive all the way. There's quite a hike once I leave the truck."

"You like it there?"

"Yeah. It's peaceful. I've always enjoyed the mountains."

"Would you show me where you live?"

His grin was unexpected. He so rarely smiled...and she'd never heard him laugh in all the years she'd known him. She blinked in surprise at the change his smile made. He was much more approachable. And devastatingly attractive.

"I'm afraid you wouldn't get far in that outfit."

He hadn't said no. "I brought other clothes with me," she offered. "When Woody told me you lived in an isolated mountain area, I came prepared to look for you, no matter where you were."

He hadn't expected that, she could tell. She hurried on before he could speak. "If you'll give me time to change my clothes, I'd very much like to see where you live. I also brought several reports that I'd like you to read. They can show you much better than anything I can say exactly what's been happening to the company these past months.'' She looked away for a moment before returning her gaze to him once more. ''I would also like to have a chance to change your mind about coming back to work at CPI.''

''You think spending the night with me is going to convince me?''

She could feel her cheeks warm with color. ''That's not what I meant and you know it. You know me better than that, Jake.''

''What makes you say that? I don't know you at all, 'Becca.'' He didn't need to add that he had no intention of remedying the situation. It was in his tone of voice.

''Let me show you the reports before you turn me down, Jake. If nothing else, give me your thoughts on what could be done to protect us from what's occurring in the plant. I freely admit that I don't know where to turn or what else to do. Looking for you is my last, desperate attempt to hang on to the company.''

He scratched his chin thoughtfully. Her offer to go home with him intrigued him, damned if it didn't. It was totally out of character for the woman he thought she was. But then, he'd been correct in saying he didn't know her.

Brock Adams was dead and his company was up for grabs. Jake could just see what his sudden reappearance might do to a few people he recalled who spent their working days jockeying for more powerful positions in the company. The thought made him smile slightly.

Her gaze never left his face. When he realized how hopefully she was watching him, he said, "There's a rest room through those doors—" he nodded his head toward an opening in the back wall "—where you can change clothes. Hope you brought some hiking boots."

She needed no more urging. With quick strides she hurried to the door and out to the parking lot. He watched as she disappeared from view, then shook his head. He must be more lonesome than he thought to even consider the idea of taking Rebecca Adams up to his mountain retreat.

No one had ever been there before. He'd deliberately chosen a small meadow area that could be reached only through a narrow hidden canyon. Why, after all these years, was he willing to share it with another person?

And why her?

Once Rebecca returned from the car carrying a small bag, Jake pulled out his wallet and walked over to where Betty worked behind the counter. They both watched Rebecca go into the rest room before Betty looked back at Jake.

"Nice-looking woman."

Jake placed a couple of bills on the counter. "I suppose."

"Put that back in your wallet. You know your money's no good here."

"I thought we'd managed to get past that nonsense. Does that mean I've gotta keep stashing money around the place for you to find once you close? You know good and well I'm not going to let you feed me for nothing.''

Betty sighed. "You're so blamed stubborn, you make a mule seem downright cooperative.''

He pulled on his coat and slipped his sunglasses over his eyes. "But you love me, anyway, and you know it.''

"Never said I didn't. So what's this lady doing here, did she say?''

"Guess she must have missed me,'' he replied, grinning.

"She seems a little nervous.''

"You think so? I can't imagine Ms. Adams has ever been less than completely composed.''

"Then you missed the fact that her hands were trembling the first time she picked up her cup of coffee.''

"She's had a long day. Flew in from Seattle this morning.''

"She heading back now?''

He crossed his arms over his chest. "Uh-uh. I'm takin' her home with me.''

During their conversation, Betty was wiping down the countertop, straightening each item along the way, but his last words caused her to jerk her head up.

"What did you say?'' She stared at him with widened eyes.

"You heard me.''

She looked at him, looked at the rest room door, then back at him. "I heard you. I just don't believe you.''

"Suit yourself.''

"Why would you take her up there?"

His smile couldn't be more innocent. "Because she wants to see how I live."

"A lotta folks have wanted to see how you live and where you live, and I ain't seen you selling tickets for the privilege."

He shrugged. "Maybe I'm getting bored. A little company might be nice for a change. Is it all right if we leave her rental car in the parking lot? I'll bring her back tomorrow."

Betty closed her mouth, suddenly realizing it had been hanging open since his announcement. "I would never have believed her the kind of woman to do such a thing."

"Oh, for crying out loud, Betty. She hasn't sold herself into slavery. What are you thinking? That I'll get her up there and take advantage of her? Hell, she isn't even my type!"

Betty leaned her elbows on the counter in front of her and raised her eyebrows. "I was talking about the long hike you've always gone to great lengths to describe to me. What are *you* talking about?"

Jake reached for his hat—still lying where he'd put it when he'd arrived hours ago—and settled it on his head. He tugged the brim down so it rested just above his glasses.

"She thinks she can do it. I'm willing to let her try."

They both turned when they heard the door open and watched her walk toward them, carrying her small bag. The businesswoman was gone. In her place was what looked to be a seasoned hiker, if her small boots were any indication. They'd seen plenty of use, as had the jeans that fit her so well. She wore an unzipped windbreaker over a bulky sweater.

"Sorry to take so long," she said, pausing beside him and gazing up at his hat. "I don't think I would have recognized you in your hat and sunshades."

"Hell, 'Becca, you didn't recognize me without 'em."

She glanced at Betty and gave a small shrug. "That's true. I didn't. I'd only seen him in suits before today."

"We'll leave your car here and you'll come with me in my truck. We better get a move on, so we don't run out of light." Jake opened the screen door and ushered Rebecca out. He glanced over at Betty and winked. "See you later."

Betty walked over to the screen door and watched as Jake opened the passenger door of the truck and steadied Rebecca as she climbed inside. She heard Mel come out of the kitchen and walk up behind her. "Whaddaya think?" she asked as the truck headed back down the highway toward the mountains.

"I think our boy's just met his match and don't know it."

She turned around and, laughing, hugged her man. "It's gonna be fun watchin' how it all turns out, though. Bet he's not goin' to know what hit him before all this is done."

Mel gave her a smacking kiss and returned her hug. "Us poor men never do."

Three

————

Jake glanced at Rebecca out of the corner of his eye once they were on the highway. She sat comfortably in his pickup truck, looking as regal as if she were in the back of a limousine.

He returned his attention to the road. The turnoff was unmarked, and he could easily miss it if he wasn't paying attention.

He wasn't certain what had prompted him to agree to Rebecca's suggestion. Boredom maybe. Perhaps there was a hint of malice, as well. If she wasn't willing to take his word for it that the trip to his place wasn't for a city dweller, then he guessed she'd have to see for herself.

He'd never cared for Rebecca, although he'd kept

his thoughts and feelings to himself. He'd been surprised when she'd admitted that he made her nervous. The truth was that he didn't like the kind of woman he'd taken her to be—rich, spoiled and used to getting her own way. Now he was wondering if he'd been a little quick to stick a label on her.

Brock had thought his little darlin' could do no wrong, and Jake had grown weary of hearing her virtues extolled. The only time Brock had hinted that he would like to see Rebecca and Jake as a couple Jake had quickly set Brock straight. He'd been hired to work in the company, not to participate in establishing a family dynasty.

At least Brock hadn't pursued that particular subject. Jake couldn't help but wonder what Brock would have thought about Rebecca's going to such lengths to save the company that she would seek him out. Jake had a hunch the older man would have voiced strong disapproval had he known.

Actually, her decision to seek help showed good sense. Jake wondered why Brock hadn't hired someone to replace him. Maybe he hadn't had time. From the sound of things, all hell had broken loose soon after he'd left, which didn't surprise him in the least. Hadn't he warned Brock that some of his policies and competitive decisions weren't worth the risks they were taking? Somehow, recognizing his I-told-you-so attitude didn't make him feel a hell of a lot better. Nor did he want to rush back to Seattle in his savior suit to right all the wrongs that had been committed in the name of big business.

Jake slowed the truck and turned onto the dirt road that would take them on the next stage of their journey.

"You okay?" he finally asked when he realized she hadn't spoken since they'd left the café.

She glanced around at him as though surprised to see him sitting there, before she returned her gaze to their surroundings. "Yes. I've never seen mountains like these before. They're so stark and forbidding."

"They're a far cry from the picture-postcard look of the snowcapped Cascades, that's for sure."

After a moment she nodded. "That's true, but still—they're quite majestic in their own way."

Jake realized he was pleased that she could see the beauty of the mountains. He felt like a parent showing off a child. A twinge of guilt caused him to ask, "Have you done much hiking?"

"Not lately, I'm afraid. I used to spend my summer vacations in the mountains whenever I could. However, these past few years haven't given me much free time."

At least that explained the well-used look of her hiking boots. He cleared his throat. "You're going to recognize the test of this place once we're on our feet and climbing. We want to get to my place before dark. Otherwise it's too dangerous to be moving around up there."

He shifted into lower gear as the winding road began to climb into the foothills.

"What made you decide to live up here?"

He gave her a quick glance before saying, "Like you, while growing up, I spent my summers in the mountains. I used to worry my mother by disappearing up there for days.''

She turned in her seat, pulling one knee up so that she was facing him. "Tell me about your mother. Which one of the Abbots is she related to?"

Jake had never liked talking about himself. Most especially, he'd never been one to discuss his family. So what was he supposed to say in reply? It was obvious that Rebecca was attempting to establish a line of communication between them.

Once again, he wished he hadn't agreed to bring her back with him. He let out a gusty sigh. "Neither." When he glanced her way he saw her confusion. Hell, it wasn't a deep, dark secret, his past. He'd just never considered it anyone else's business.

Jake cleared his throat, then said, "My mother was a Jicarilla Apache." His voice still sounded gruff. He swallowed, frowned, then continued. "She made the mistake of falling in love with the wrong guy and married him despite her family's objections. When he abandoned her she refused to return to her people. Mel and Betty ended up taking her in and giving her a place to live."

She didn't say anything immediately and Jake held a brief hope that her curiosity was satisfied. He should have known better.

"How old were you when your father left?" she asked after several minutes of silence.

His short laugh showed no amusement. "I was little more than a dream in my mother's thoughts. No one ever said anything to me, but I figure he must have left when he found out she was pregnant."

She looked out the window as they rounded a sharp curve, watching the primitive road. Quietly she asked, "Did he ever return?"

"No."

"So you never knew your father," she murmured in the silence of the truck's cab. He was relieved not to hear pity or sympathy in her voice and found himself relaxing slightly.

"Never wanted to," he immediately responded. "My mother didn't deserve that kind of treatment."

"So Mr. Abbott was a surrogate father for you?"

Jake mulled that one over for several minutes, recalling his childhood. "I suppose. My mother worked there at the café until she died."

"How old were you when she died?"

He gave her a brief glance of irritation. Damn, but the woman was inquisitive! "Ten."

Once again she sounded matter-of-fact when she said, "It's tough losing a parent, no matter how old you are. I was already in my twenties when my mother died, and it was still a devastating blow. Even then I had my father. It's a wonder you survived as well as you did."

He pulled off the dirt road he'd been following and parked the truck in a sheltered place by a stone overhang.

"She did what she could for me," he admitted. "And, as you pointed out, I had the Abbotts." He turned off the engine and looked over at her. "Figure out what you want to take with you up there—" he nodded toward the surrounding peaks "—and I'll carry it in here." He opened the truck door and

stepped out, then reached behind the seat for a rucksack.

Rebecca quickly got out on her side and reached for
her bag and brief case. "Oh, that's all right. I can
carry them."

He shook his head. "I have only one backpack and
it's too heavy for you. You'll need your hands free."

For the first time since he'd seen her walk into the
café Rebecca Adams looked unsure of herself. He almost smiled at the expression on her face. "I warned
you that it wouldn't be easy getting to my place."

She nodded. "I know you did, but I thought there
would be a trail to follow and that we would be hiking."

"I've never wanted anyone to know where the place
is, so I've deliberately used different ways to reach the
narrow canyon that leads into the meadow." He could
have taken her on one of the easier routes, but he
chose not to. He didn't want her deciding she could
find the place on her own some other time and try to
come back for another attempt to persuade him to return to Seattle.

She turned to her bag and opened it, frowning.

"If you want to change your mind, now's the time.
I can still take you back down to the café. You can
spend the night at Mel and Betty's and—"

"No. I mean, that's all right, I can do this." She
sorted through some clothing, then reluctantly handed
him a few items when he joined her on the passenger
side of the truck. He stuffed them into the backpack
while she opened her briefcase and gathered up the
files. Silently she handed them to him. Without

glancing at them, he opened a side flap and slid the files into the pocket, then carefully made sure the top closed.

After adjusting the rucksack and its straps, he made certain the doors were all locked on the truck, then looked around at Rebecca. "Ready?"

She stood with her hands tucked in her windbreaker pockets, gazing at the rough terrain. With a slight shrug and a smile, she nodded. "As ready as I'll ever be. Something tells me I'm going to be sorry I skipped some of my gym workouts this winter."

He almost smiled. She was being a better sport about this than he'd expected. He felt another twinge of guilt, but only for a moment. He had to remember who she was and why she had come to Texas. He couldn't afford to allow her any advantages where he was concerned.

Without comment he turned and headed up into the next phase of their journey.

Rebecca didn't know how long they'd been following what appeared to her as a nonexistent trail. She'd been too busy keeping up with Jake's long-legged pace. He wasn't even breathing hard and he was wearing a backpack. She, on the other hand, sounded like a steam engine in dire straits.

For some reason she'd pictured her visit to the mountains as a long drive along a primitive road, followed by a hike of several hundred feet to Jake's home. Instead, she was thoroughly confused with all the twists and turns they had taken since leaving the truck.

Despite her lungs' strenuous objections, she was determined to show Jake that she had the stamina and willingness to follow him back into his hidden mountain lair. Too bad she hadn't understood just how accurate a description that had turned out to be.

She was so wrapped up in her thoughts that when Jake halted she almost ran into him.

"You okay?" he asked gruffly.

If she'd had any wind left, she would have laughed. Instead, she took the respite to draw much-needed air into her lungs. "Just dandy," she finally managed to wheeze.

He frowned. "If I was going too fast you should have said something."

She leaned over, bracing her arms against her bent knees, while she continued to take deep breaths. When she finally straightened she looked him in the eye and said, "But that was the whole point in this exercise, wasn't it? To show me how out of place I am in your world?"

She noted a slight ruddiness spread across his high cheekbones. Hah! At least he had the grace to blush. She looked around them but saw nothing that looked like a dwelling. A narrow canyon branched off to the left of where they were standing.

He nodded toward the canyon. "We need to go that way. We're almost there."

Her knees had the consistency of gelatin. Only her sheer determination not to allow him to win this round gave her enough energy to lift her chin and say, "Okay."

"The worst of the climb is behind us. You did well, better than many seasoned climbers."

"Does that mean I passed one of your tests?"

He grinned, darn him, which didn't help the consistency of her knees at all. "I did warn you, you know," he pointed out quite reasonably.

Too bad she was fast losing her reasonable mood. "So you did." She glanced around them and added, "The light's fading fast, isn't it?"

He eyed her for a moment in silence before taking the lead once more.

The canyon continued to narrow until they came to the end of it. How strange, she thought. Why would he lead her down a blind canyon? Was he hoping she would make loud objections to the unnecessary journey? Too bad. She was learning a few things about Jake Taggart. By the same token, he was going to learn a few things about her as well. She could be as tenacious as he was. She knew what her objective was, and she didn't intend to back down from it. However, there was a good chance she'd be too stiff tomorrow to walk out of the mountains.

A sudden picture of him carrying her out slung over the top of the backpack almost made her laugh out loud.

Jake's pace didn't slacken as he continued toward the blank surface of the canyon wall. He paused by a thicket growing alongside the wall and waited for her to join him. He nodded toward a gaping black hole hidden behind the thicket. "You can go ahead now. There's only one way to go. You can't get lost."

She stared up at him in disbelief. "Are you telling me you brought building materials through here?"

"No. There's another way in, but it would have taken us two more hours to go that way. This is the most direct route."

But obviously not the easiest, she realized. They had been steadily climbing without a break, taking the most direct route upward at every turn. Tentatively she edged toward the black hole. "Is this a cave?" she asked, and realized that she was whispering.

In a normal tone he answered, "Yes. It links this area to the other side."

As soon as she stepped inside she paused to allow her eyes to adjust to the darkness. A faint light glowed in the distance, and she discovered that she could see better than she'd guessed she would.

"Here," Jake said from behind her, and she turned. He handed her a flashlight. It was small but gave off adequate light for her to watch her footing. She hurried toward the source of light in the distance. She could almost feel the weight of the mountain above her, pressing down on all sides.

When she stepped out of the cave onto a wide ledge she couldn't contain her gasp of surprise. This must have been the way the world looked when it was freshly formed. The mountain walls surrounded a perfect valley of trees and grass, with a stream rushing along, bouncing and bubbling across smooth stones and disappearing beneath the mountain once again.

Deer grazed along the edge of the stream. The buck watched them as Jake joined her on the ledge while several doe continued to eat. "They don't look afraid," she whispered.

"No reason. They're used to me."

He started down a narrow trail that had been chiseled along the edge of the canyon wall until it reached the floor of the meadow. Rebecca caught her breath at the ease with which he moved down the dangerous looking path. He made it look so easy.

She placed her hand against the side and slowly followed him, leaning away from the sharp drop. It was only when she reached the bottom that she remembered to breathe.

"I've never seen a place so beautiful," she murmured. "No wonder you returned here."

"It's a healing place," he said without looking at her.

"Yes." She knew what he meant. The air seemed to shimmer with clarity. Colors appeared brighter, sounds sharper.

Jake's stride lengthened once again as he cut across the center of the meadow toward the back canyon wall. Her muscles protested the new pace, and she tried to dismiss the pain by concentrating on her surroundings. The meadow was truly beautiful, its lushness surprising at this time of year and in these barren mountains.

They were almost upon it before Rebecca saw the cabin. It was built into the rock itself, blending into the natural contour of its surroundings. There was a window on either side of the door and an overhanging roof that sheltered a small porch.

"It looks enchanted."

She didn't realize she'd spoken her thoughts aloud until he laughed and looked around at her.

Damn him and his attractive smile. She didn't need the tug of awareness that shot through her every time he allowed her a glimpse of the whimsical boy hidden deep within the stern man.

He opened the door and stepped inside, holding it for her. There was an expectancy about him that triggered her curiosity. As soon as she crossed the threshold, she understood why.

The place was much larger than she had suspected. Jake had obviously built his cabin inside a large cave, carefully adding materials so that the floor, ceiling and walls were covered and sealed. The windows caught the western light, flooding the room with dancing motes of sunshine. The floor was smoothly planed and sanded and shone like golden glass.

She walked over to the table and touched it lightly with her fingertips. "Did you make this?"

He nodded. "I made all the furniture. It's sort of a hobby of mine."

She looked around at the four-poster bed, the matching chairs, the kitchen area with the roomy cupboard space and shook her head. "This isn't my idea of roughing it in the outdoors."

He shrugged. "I have a generator that keeps the refrigerator going, but I use kerosene lanterns for light and I cook on the woodburning stove."

She slowly turned around in the middle of the room, seeing the loving attention to detail that was displayed. "You've never shown this to anyone?" she finally asked.

He frowned at the question, before suddenly busying himself with removing the backpack and unloading it. "No," he finally replied without looking at her.

That's when it occurred to her that she was looking at the entire cabin. "No plumbing, I take it," she offered dryly.

"No guest room, either," he replied in the same tone.

She shrugged. "That's no problem. If you have a bedroll I can—"

"No, you can't. You'll take the bed, of course. In the summertime I generally sleep outdoors, anyway."

"May I point out that this isn't summertime."

"I know. But I'm used to camping out, sleeping on whatever surface is available. You aren't." He handed her the clothes and files she'd given him at the truck.

She took them without comment. It didn't matter, anyway. The point was that she was here now. She couldn't believe her luck. She forgot her aches and pains in the knowledge that she was actually with Jake. She'd accomplished her first goal. She'd found him.

She'd known it wasn't going to be easy to convince him to return, but she was bolstered by the fact that he'd made an exception in her case by allowing her to visit his mountain home.

That must mean something, even though she wasn't quite certain what.

She would have to play out the scene one step at a time. Somehow, someway, she had to convince him that he had to return to Seattle.

She needed him—for the good of the company, of course.

Four

Rebecca was relieved to discover that the skills she'd developed during her earlier hiking and camping experiences came back to her and she was able to help Jake prepare their meal. He'd lit the kerosene lamps once the sunlight was blocked by the high cliffs surrounding the meadow.

She'd even been able to be nonchalant when he'd shown her the latrine he'd constructed not too far away.

Now they companionably cleared the table and washed their dishes with some of the water he'd brought in from the stream earlier. He'd filled a large pot sitting on the back of the stove so that the water was heated by the time they needed it.

"It's like living in another century, isn't it?" she said, her voice sounding loud after the silence that had seemed to wrap around them like an unseen presence. She hadn't noticed the silence until it was broken, because she'd been comfortable with the routine they had unconsciously fallen into.

Rebecca was startled by the insight. She never would have believed she could be so at ease around Jake Taggart, at least, not the one she thought she knew.

But this Jake was not the same man—he neither looked like him nor acted like him, although admittedly Jake had never been one to talk much.

"I suppose," he acknowledged, carefully folding the drying towel he'd been using. "I suppose it makes a change from what you're used to."

He hadn't looked at her, but there was a new edge to his voice, one that was reminiscent of the Jake she had known in Seattle.

She crossed her arms, folding them around her waist. "Yes," she agreed slowly, "I doubt that many people living in cities today could imagine a place like this."

He turned away from the kitchen area and went over to the potbellied stove. After checking the fire, he placed several more pieces of wood inside.

"Jake, you've made it clear that you have little use for me, but at least keep an open mind when you look through the files I brought. I'm not asking you to like me, or approve of me, but if you have any feeling for what the company meant to my dad, you'll at least read the reports."

His jaw tightened as he stood from his kneeling position in front of the stove. He looked at her for a long moment, then away. He shoved his hand through his hair.

"Look, 'Becca. I'm not exactly proud of myself for dragging you up here. You've been a good sport about it. I guess my little prank backfired on me. I fully expected you to demand that we go back before we ever reached the valley."

His eyes appeared even darker in the soft lamplight.

"Are you apologizing to me?"

Jake's gaze didn't waver. "Yeah. I guess I am."

She smiled. "Guess we've both learned something. I never expected to hear you admit to being wrong about anything."

"I've been wrong about a lot of things."

"Like leaving CPI?"

He turned away from her, picked up a chair and joined her in front of the warm stove before answering. "No. I can't say that leaving was wrong. Maybe the way I did it, but my reasons were sound."

"Tell me about them."

He stared at her for a long time before replying. "It wasn't because of any one thing, it was because of the philosophy behind the business. I don't mind taking risks, but not at the expense of people's lives!"

She sat forward. "What are you talking about?"

He got up, as though too restless to sit still. He walked to the window and looked out, although she was certain he could see nothing but the night past the reflected light of the lamps. He'd stuck his hands in the back pockets of his jeans, calling her attention to their snug fit.

She blinked, then glanced away from his lean, muscled figure.

"The government was pushing us to provide parts for an experimental craft," he finally said, still facing the window. "There was to be some kind of hearing, and they wanted to be able to produce positive results in order to keep their funding."

She waited, but he didn't say any more. Jake was finally talking to her, finally letting her into his life in a way she hadn't been sure he would ever do. In no way did she want to distract him.

Finally he said, "I told Brock that we hadn't tested one of the parts sufficiently. That we needed more time, regardless of the pressure. He insisted that we'd done enough."

"So the flight went as scheduled..." she finally said softly.

"And the pilot was killed," he said, finishing her sentence.

"Did it crash because of the untested part?"

He shrugged. "I don't know. The crash was still being investigated when I left." He turned and looked at her. "At that point it no longer mattered to me. I'd told Brock what I thought. He brushed away my objections, saying that we couldn't afford to offend our biggest customer by delaying production of our parts. He was willing to allow the government to be accountable for their decisions."

"You disagreed."

"Of course the government is accountable for what they do. All I was saying was that CPI needed to accept responsibility and accountability for what we produced and the conditions surrounding our production."

"Do you think the part was defective?"

Once again he ran his hand through his hair. "God, I hope not! I've spent a lot of sleepless nights wondering—wondering if we could have saved the pilot's life, if we could have delayed enough to make absolutely certain—"

He walked over to the refrigerator and pulled out a beer. Holding it up to her, he silently offered her one. She shook her head. He removed the cap and took a long drink before joining her in front of the fire once more. "That was a year ago. I'm sure they know more about the matter now."

"If you come back, Jake, you will be in charge of all decisions with regard to manufacturing and testing products."

He glanced at her. "If I came back, I'd insist upon it."

She got up from where she'd sat watching him and walked over to the bed where she'd placed the files. Silently she handed them to him.

"What do you want me to do with these?" he asked, looking at them suspiciously.

She smiled. "Read them, of course."

"I'm no longer associated with the company, 'Becca. I have no business looking at classified documents."

She sighed and shook her head. "Damn, but you're stubborn. If I thought you were going to steal company secrets I wouldn't be here in the first place, Jake. These reports cover the last twelve months and will tell you more concisely and precisely than I can where we stand and why I'm here. Please look at them."

He stared at her for a long moment before he slowly reached to take the files in question. He dropped them on the table in front of him, propped his booted foot on the edge of the table and pushed his chair back so that it was balanced on the two back legs. Then he picked up the first file and flipped it open.

She watched him become engrossed almost immediately in what he was reading. She wasn't at all surprised. According to her father, this man had an uncanny head for business details, for visualizing what was happening to the operations of the company by scanning reports.

While he read, she looked around the snug cabin once again. She could see the hard physical labor that had gone into making the place as comfortable as it was. His attention to detail was another trait that made him good at whatever he set out to do.

Quietly she got up and slipped into her jacket before she walked over to the door. When she opened it, he looked up. "You want me to go with you?"

She looked out at the black night. The light cast by the lamps shining through the windows formed squares of glowing yellow on the ground. Past the comforting light she could see nothing but blackness.

"Are there animals out there?"

His smile was lopsided. "You won't get mugged, but yes, there are some predators that might consider you a tasty morsel for an evening snack."

She swallowed, looking out into the blackness. There were some definite drawbacks to a primitive Eden.

"Then, yes, I'd like you to go with me. Thank you."

"No problem." He dropped the chair back on all four legs and stood, grabbed his denim jacket, then followed her out the door.

The air was crisp and cold now that the sun no longer warmed it. Rebecca inhaled, astonished at how clean and clear everything seemed to her. Once away from the cabin, the night no longer seemed so black. She looked up and saw the sky overhead was full of brilliant stars. They looked so close that she felt as though all she would have to do to touch them was to scale the walls of the surrounding cliffs and stand on tiptoe.

"Oh, Jake. This is so beautiful." She kept her voice hushed.

"Yeah," he finally answered in a gruff tone.

"Do you ever wish we could take off and visit all those twinkling lights? Do you ever wonder if there are others like us, seeing us as a twinkling light, wondering if they're alone in the universe?"

She saw his shadowy figure pause, his face turn to her. She couldn't see his expression. "Never gave it much thought," he admitted, looking up. "I suppose it makes sense that we aren't the only ones around."

When they reached the small outbuilding he took her hand and placed a cylindrical object in it. "I brought a flashlight for you to use once you get inside, just to make sure you don't have any company."

She shivered as he placed the light in her hands. She hesitated, not wanting to turn it on and reduce the beauty of the night with artificial light. The moonlight cast a silvery sheen across the meadow, guiding her steps, while Jake waited beside one of the trees, saying, "I'll wait here. You'll be safe enough if anything should show up."

She took the flashlight with her, but waited until she opened the door to the small shelter before turning it on. She didn't want anything waiting for her inside there, either.

When she got ready to leave, she turned off the light and stepped back out into the silvery enchantment of the night.

Instead of returning to the cabin, Jake silently took her hand and led her in the other direction, toward the stream. He drew her beneath the blackness of the trees and nodded toward the water.

At first she didn't see anything. She was too conscious of the fact that he had nonchalantly wrapped his arms around her and pulled her back against his chest, enfolding her in his warmth. He rested his chin on the crown of her head, seemingly content to lean against the tree with her in his arms.

She could feel her heart racing. She never knew what this man was going to do next! Standing stiffly in his arms she tried to appear relaxed while she wondered why he'd brought her here. Then a movement caught her eye and she squinted, trying to see through the enveloping darkness beneath the trees.

She saw a procession of small night creatures venturing down to the water. When she leaned away to look up at Jake, he nodded and smiled. Fascinated, Rebecca returned her gaze to the watering hole and watched in silent awe as various animals performed what must be a nightly routine.

When they suddenly scattered, she waited to see what had startled them. A darker, much larger shadow silently moved along a path to the bank. She held her breath as she watched the animal drink, then disappear back into the undergrowth without making a sound.

She shivered, and Jake silently drew her away from the stream and led her back to the cabin. He continued to hold her hand until they reached the door.

As soon as they were inside, she turned to him. "How did you know they would be there?"

"I know their habits, their feeding places. They're part of my environment, as I'm part of theirs."

"You mean they knew we were there?"

"Yes."

"And they didn't mind?"

"Not as long as we were still. If we'd made any threatening moves, they would have disappeared in a flash."

She smiled at him, determined to ignore the feelings he'd invoked by holding her in his arms. "Thank you for sharing all of this with me."

"It's the least I could do since I dragged you up here."

"I volunteered, remember?"

"Without having a clue what you were getting yourself into."

"True enough." She rubbed the front of her thighs. "My muscles are already stiffening up on me. I probably won't be able to move tomorrow."

He nodded toward the bed. "You're welcome to go on to bed."

She looked longingly at the bed. "You wouldn't mind?"

He shook his head. "I'll give you some privacy," he motioned to the door. "If the light won't bother you, I think I'll continue looking at the files you brought with you. I'll admit you have me intrigued."

She almost hugged him. He stood there, his hand still on the door, wearing his denim jacket with the collar turned up, not looking at all like the corporate officer who could save her company if he only agreed to return. He seemed to be a mass of contradictions to her.

"I doubt that anything will keep me awake once I get into bed," she admitted, grinning.

With a nod, he opened the door and stepped outside, leaving her alone.

She wasted no time in slipping out of her clothes and changing into warm pajamas before getting beneath the covers with a sigh. The heat from the stove made the room feel cozy, and she almost groaned aloud with the pleasure of finally being able to stretch out and allow her muscles to relax.

She sank into the comforting softness of the bed and closed her eyes, vaguely aware of a new sense of well-

being that had been absent from her life for a long
time.

Jake stood in the shadows and watched the wildlife
continue to move toward the rippling stream. He was
shaken by the realization that he was enjoying sharing his retreat from the world with Rebecca. She'd
continued to surprise him all afternoon as she'd
gamely followed him into the mountains, pushing
herself to stay up with him.

He'd been as guilty of stereotyping a person as he'd
once felt stereotyped. He'd allowed his experiences at
college to color his views toward any woman who had
been brought up with all the privileges money can buy.

He'd seen Rebecca through the distorted lens of his
past experiences. The unexpected insight into his own
motives and character didn't make him feel very good.
In fact, he felt lousy.

In addition, he'd made the uncomfortable discovery while holding her in his arms that he was physically attracted to her. Given their isolated intimacy, the
timing of his discovery wasn't the greatest.

Now he had to go back to the cabin and ignore the
fact that she was cosily tucked into his bed. Silently
moving away from the water, Jake headed back to the
cabin. He'd had long enough to look at the reports
she'd brought to understand that the company was
headed for serious trouble unless something was done
very quickly.

He pushed the door open and noted that Rebecca
appeared to be sound asleep. No doubt she'd wake up
with stiff muscles after their hike. He pushed away the

guilt he felt, knowing there was little he could do about it now.

Instead, he allowed the uncomfortable feeling to spur him into returning to the reports she'd been so determined that he study. At least he could tell her in the morning that he had read them and perhaps make some suggestions to help during the transition period, before sending her back to Seattle.

Hours later he wearily rubbed his eyes and balefully stared at the reports scattered across the table. If Brock had had any idea— Well, it was pointless to speculate on what Brock would have done, but at least Rebecca's motives for seeking him out were much clearer. Jake knew that he was the only one who could fully understand what Brock had been doing with the company, where he had been guiding it and what he had hoped to accomplish.

Someone was working diligently to destroy the company. If he could find out who, he would probably know why. Or vice versa.

Despite all his reservations, he was intrigued enough to consider returning to Seattle to do some investigating. Not on a permanent basis, of course. Just long enough to physically inspect what the documents were reporting. Costs were rising, production was falling off, unexplained accidents were happening with alarming frequency, and nobody seemed to have any answers to offer to the new owner of the company.

Rebecca was absolutely right. She was way over her head. He had several questions that hadn't been answered by what he'd found in the files.

He wanted to know when all of this had started. He wanted to know what Brock had been working on when he'd died, and he especially wanted to know what had happened to the project that had caused him to leave the company. Wouldn't it be ironic if Brock had—in the end—taken his advice even though he'd already left? Knowing Brock, he would have had too much pride to admit it. From the sound of things, it was probably that stiff-necked pride that had killed him. Rather than admit he needed help, he'd tried to do it all on his own.

Jake stood and stretched, glancing over at the sleeping woman in his bed. She had slept soundly these past several hours, scarcely moving. He turned away and restoked the fire in the potbelly stove before spreading his bedroll nearby. After blowing out the kerosene lantern he stretched out on his makeshift bed and immediately fell into an exhausted sleep.

Sometime later the whisper of an unidentifiable noise brought him from a sound sleep. Like an animal who had learned to survive in the wilds, his finely attuned senses had relayed an unfamiliar presence. He opened his eyes without betraying his sudden shift in consciousness and immediately recognized what his subconscious had forgotten. He had a visitor.

In the soft light of early dawn his gaze sharpened and focused on the visible form of the woman standing beside his bed, removing her pajamas. She was turned away from him in semiprofile so that he was given the unobstructed view of her scantily covered back and hips. She wore a translucent pair of lace briefs. As he watched, she turned so that he glimpsed her breasts when she reached for her bra.

He closed his eyes, suddenly conscious of the fact that he was staring unabashedly at her while she thought he lay asleep. What the hell was wrong with him, anyway? It wasn't as if he hadn't seen a well-shaped woman before, although he was honest enough to admit that it had been several months. He already knew that Rebecca's trim body was alluring. He didn't want to think of her as a woman at the moment, not after his decision last night. If she was going to be his employer, even for a limited amount of time, he needed to keep the relationship on a purely professional level.

The last thing he needed, given their present situation, was to feel the strong tug of physical attraction that had hit him last night.

He turned over onto his side, his back to her. He needed to get up, even though he'd only had a few hours sleep. He'd give her a few minutes before he let her know he was awake.

The door to the cabin quietly opened, then closed. He rolled onto his back and confirmed that she had slipped outside. Jake forced himself out of the warm cocoon of his sleeping bag and stretched. He reached for his jeans and shirt and quickly dressed, then walked over to the stove. The wood he'd placed in there earlier was still providing enough heat to take the chill off the room. After putting coffee on, he opened one of his large storage cabinets and pulled out his luggage.

When Rebecca entered the cabin several minutes later, he was filling his larger case with what he thought of as his city clothes.

"Boy! Is it cold out there," she began as she hastily closed the door behind her. "Frost is everywhere and there're some heavy clouds rolling in." She had reached the stove and was holding her hands over it when she saw his open luggage. "Jake?" Her voice sounded surprised and happy. "Have you changed your mind? Are you going to come back to CPI?"

He didn't look up. "Not on a permanent basis, but I'll see what I can do to help you deal with what's going on. You don't have too many people in your corner at the moment."

She walked over to him and waited until he looked at her. "I can't tell you how much this means to me, Jake. I wouldn't have known what else to do if you'd been determined to stay here."

He had trouble meeting her gaze. "Hopefully it won't take long. Someone is systematically working to destroy the company. Once I find out who it is, you shouldn't have any trouble keeping things running smoothly."

She gave a small laugh. "I'm not proud, Jake. I'll take whatever you are willing to offer." She looked at his luggage. "I take it you mean to go back with me?"

He paused and walked over to the window. "Yeah. I thought we could leave right after breakfast, but now I'm not so sure." He pulled his jacket on. "I'd better see how the weather's shaping up before making any kind of decision."

Her eyes widened. "You mean we may have to stay here longer?"

He glanced over his shoulder and saw that the idea didn't please her any more than it did him, but he was sure her reason wasn't the same as his. She didn't care for the primitive facilities, while he didn't need to be reminded that he was sharing an isolated cabin with a very attractive woman. If there were any way possible for them to leave today, he'd do it. However, an unexpected storm at these higher elevations could cause havoc. There was no sense in risking their lives.

"I'll know better once I've checked," he muttered as he stepped outside, closing the door behind him.

Rebecca saw that Jake had made coffee and gratefully poured herself a cup. Then she began to gather ingredients to prepare breakfast.

She'd slept wonderfully well. In fact, she couldn't remember when she'd had a better night's sleep. If Jake was willing to come back to Seattle with her, then she hoped they could leave before he changed his mind.

Yet, it had been all she could do to get out of bed that morning. Every muscle in her body had protested each movement. So she really wouldn't mind having a chance to rest up before starting the arduous trek back to the truck.

She had bacon frying and biscuits in the oven when Jake came in along with a flurry of cold, damp air. He stamped his boots and hung his coat on one of the knobs along the wall.

"Doesn't seem to be warming up, anyway," she offered, pouring him a cup of coffee and handing it to him.

He shook his head in disgust. "No. It's beginning to sleet."

"Oh."

He looked around the room, then back at her. "I don't want to take a chance on getting caught on the trail in this kind of stuff."

She nodded. "Okay."

"It should clear in a few hours. Maybe by this afternoon we will be able to get out of here."

"Fine." She motioned him to the table and set a plate filled with steaming food in front of him.

"You don't appear too worried about getting stranded up here."

She smiled. "I'm not." She looked around the warm room and added, "We should be safe enough here."

He looked disgruntled. "Of course we're safe, but we'll be wasting time sitting here. I wanted to get to El Paso today. We'll need to book a flight to Seattle. I want to show up at the company before anyone has an idea I'm coming."

"Don't worry. After Woody's unsuccessful trip looking for you, nobody will be expecting you to show up so quickly after I left."

He leaned back in his chair a little. "That's a point."

"Do you think it's someone in the company, Jake?"

"Absolutely. Have you had any offers to buy you out?"

She rubbed her forehead. "No."

"Then they're still trying to set you up, so that by the time a low offer is made, you'll be only too willing to accept it."

"Is that what all this is about?"

He finished everything on his plate before responding. "Count on it. Someone figures that now that Brock is out of the picture, the company is ripe for picking up for next to nothing."

"But you're not going to let them, are you?" She knew her relief showed in her voice.

"Not if I can help it."

Before she allowed herself to think about what she was doing, Rebecca moved around the table and hugged Jake. Placing a quick kiss on his cheek, she said, "I knew I could count on you. No matter what happened between you and Dad, I knew that you'd understand and would help me."

He stared at her, obviously surprised at her enthusiasm and actions. "I'm not going to stay, though," he repeated. "This is only a temporary thing, even though I don't want you to let anyone know that part of the agreement."

She nodded. "Whatever you say."

He suddenly shoved his chair back. "I'll go check the weather again," he announced quickly before he grabbed his coat and hat and left the cabin.

Rebecca stared after him, puzzled at his hurry. Hadn't he just been out there? What could have changed in such a short time? She shrugged and began to clear the table. Cleaning up the kitchen and looking at supplies for lunch should keep her busy for a while, at least.

Jake stood in the clearing, sleet striking his face like needles, wishing he hadn't been so damned smart about bringing her up there. What the hell was he going to do if they had to stay another night?

From the looks of things, there wasn't a choice. Ignoring the sleet, he strode across the meadow toward the other end where the narrow path led up to the cave entrance.

Of course it was too slippery to attempt to climb out of the enclosed valley. He'd known that before he'd checked it out.

It was time to face some truths. Number one—he'd been too long without a woman. Two—the Rebecca Adams he'd gotten to know these past couple of days was a far cry from the spoiled rich girl he'd always thought her. Three—he ached with wanting her.

Nothing like a good old-fashioned case of lust on a stormy winter day to add to an already awkward situation. All right. So he found her attractive. Big deal. He could handle it. He wasn't some green kid with no self-restraint.

So why was he standing out in an ice storm talking to himself rather than inside his cozy little cabin? Somehow that damn cabin had managed to shrink since Rebecca had arrived.

He couldn't seem to get far enough away from her. He could smell the light floral scent she wore from anywhere in the room. The lighting was never so poor that he didn't notice how her dark hair framed her face, giving her an innocent, almost otherworldly look.

Like an idiot he'd filled his view and mind with how she looked stripped down to next to nothing, so he didn't have to strain his imagination. Hell, no. He could just call up the memory in nothing flat now. No effort needed.

As if all of that wasn't enough. In her gratitude she'd had to wrap her arms around his neck and kiss him! He could still feel the soft pressure of her lips against his unshaven jaw.

He hunched his shoulders, adjusted his collar and turned back toward the cabin. He couldn't stand out here all day or he'd catch pneumonia. Of course, there was a certain similarity between the weather and a cold shower, he supposed. Effective enough to make him clench his teeth to keep them from chattering and hurry his steps to the remembered warmth of his home.

As soon as he opened the door, he realized he'd blundered again. It hadn't even occurred to him to tap on the door first. So he caught her clutching a towel that she was hastily wrapping around her body—her bare body—while she explained.

"Oh! I'm sorry. I probably should have asked first, but I wanted to clean up a little, so I took some of the heated water for a sponge bath. I thought I'd be through before you returned."

He leaned against the door and pushed the brim of his hat up with a sigh. Shaking his head, he said, "You don't owe me any apologies, 'Becca. That's what I do when it's too cold to swim in the creek." He pushed away from the door and removed his hat and coat. Keeping his back carefully turned toward her he determinedly stared out the window. "Go ahead. Don't let me stop you."

He heard her sigh of relief. The fool woman obviously trusted him more than he trusted himself. He could hear water splashing while she asked, "Is it clearing up any?"

"There's no way we're going to be able to get out of here today. The ice isn't melting. One thing about the weather in these parts—it's so quick to change that we could be under a heat wave by morning."

"Really?"

He allowed himself a small smile while he continued to face the window. "Maybe that's a slight exaggeration. Another thing we're noted for in Texas."

Now he heard a rustling of clothing. "Well," she said, her voice muffled through material, "let's hope we can leave soon. I didn't bring much to wear." Another pause. "You can turn around now. Thanks."

She was brushing her hair when he turned around. The dull light from outside was augmented by one of the lamps. She looked like a little girl freshly scrubbed, at least her face did. Her complexion glowed with youth and good health.

Jake rubbed his jaw. "Guess I'd better shave. I forgot all about it yesterday." He poured more water from the container at the back of the stove and gathered up his gear.

She sat down to watch him.

He raised a brow when he saw what she was doing, and she grinned.

"I haven't watched anyone shave since I was a little girl, when I used to tag along behind my dad."

Great. At this rate he'd probably end up nicking himself out of self-consciousness. Trying to get his mind on another subject, he said, "Surely you've had occasion to watch the men you've dated sometime in your past."

She straightened her spine. "Afraid not. Somehow they manage to pick me up at the door with that chore already accomplished."

He paused while lathering his face and looked at her. "You know what I mean. Haven't you had a weekend or two when you and a—" He stopped speaking when she began to shake her head. "No?"

"No."

"Never?"

"Never."

"I find that hard to believe." He concentrated on his face in the mirror and began to remove the shaving cream and whiskers with his razor.

"Why?"

"Because you're a very attractive woman. You're a very intelligent woman, and at the risk of sounding crass, a very wealthy woman. I'm sure that all kinds of men are—"

"I didn't say I haven't received any offers."

"Oh."

"If I thought those offers were based on the fact that they found me attractive or intelligent I might have considered them. However..." She allowed her voice to trail off.

"Not every man that looks at you sees dollar signs, I'm sure."

"Probably not. I guess the truth of the matter is that I've never met anyone that I wanted to spend that kind of time with."

He glanced around and saw that her cheeks were glowing.

"That kind of time?" he repeated.

"You know. Spend a weekend with."

"I see."

He said nothing more. Neither did she. The silence that lingered felt charged with tension. Whether either one of them wanted to verbalize it or not, the fact was that they were in a similar situation—alone in an isolated cabin—even though they hadn't set out to do more than spend a few hours up there.

Of course, Jake reminded himself, she hadn't chosen to spend the time with him because she was attracted to him. She'd made it very clear from the beginning that she had come seeking his help with regard to the company.

He couldn't allow himself to take advantage of the opportunity that had presented itself.

He wiped the remaining bits of shaving cream from his skin, splashed water on his face to make certain he'd gotten all of it off, then looked over at her.

"So what do you want to do for the rest of the day?"

He watched in astonishment as her face turned a fiery red.

* * *

Hours later Jake looked toward the window that proclaimed darkness had well and truly set in, glanced at his watch, then said, "Would you like me to accompany you outside once more before we turn in? Hopefully we can get an early start in the morning."

He watched Rebecca uncurl herself from the small rug he'd placed in front of the stove, stand and stretch. "I guess so. I can't believe how quickly the time's gone today. I can't remember when I've had so much free time to read and relax."

He'd shown her his collection of books, both nonfiction and novels, as well as some of his magazines. She'd discovered his enjoyment of mysteries and they'd discussed their favorite authors in the genre over lunch.

He'd spent as much time outside as possible, trying to maintain a necessary distance between the two of them. And now the day was drawing to a close.

Maybe he'd be able to get a little sleep.

They followed the routine set up last night. He accompanied her back to the cabin and stayed outside long enough to ensure she would be in bed. He even tapped on the door before he came back inside.

After making certain there was enough wood in the stove to keep the place warm all night, Jake crawled into his sleeping bag and finally allowed himself to relax.

"Thank you, Jake."

He raised his head but couldn't see her across the room. "For what?"

"For being such a gentleman. Some men might have taken advantage of our situation."

"Maybe."

"No. They really would have."

"Don't try to hang any haloes on me, 'Becca. They won't fit."

He heard her giggle. "Good night, Jake."

"Night, 'Becca."

But it was a long time before he finally was able to fall asleep.

Jake woke up the next morning to sunshine. Glancing over at the bed, he saw that Rebecca was still asleep. Hurriedly he got out of the sleeping bag and pulled on his jeans and shirt. As soon as he had his socks and boots on, he reached for his hat and coat and eased out the door.

The meadow glistened with rime. He took a deep breath and smiled. The sky was blue, and the sun had already started its work of melting the frost around them. Since the path to the cave had gotten the early-morning sun, he would be willing to bet that it would be dry in a couple of hours.

Then they could get out of there.

Rebecca was just stirring when he came back in to put on the coffee.

"Is the storm over?"

"Yeah. We should be able to get out of here by the time we've eaten and packed up." He didn't look around at her. "I won't turn around if you want to get dressed."

He heard the rustling of the bedclothes and the whispery sounds of clothes being pulled over soft skin.

His damned imagination was working overtime.

By the time she joined him in the kitchen area he was ready to bolt from the room once more. Instead, he stayed, and the two of them prepared a quick breakfast, then methodically packed and put out the fires in the cookstove and the heating stove.

Before Rebecca could quite believe it, they were heading across the valley to the path that led to the canyon.

Jake carried two bags as well as his backpack, still insisting that she keep her hands free. Because of the narrowness in the trail he made two trips to carry both bags, leaving one arm free to brace against the side of the cliff.

Somehow the return trip seemed so much quicker to Rebecca, partly because she had a better idea where she was going and partly because it was downhill most of the way. After the first half hour her achy muscles warmed up and began to cooperate, so that she actually enjoyed herself on the trip down.

However, she was still glad to see the truck and was disgusted to discover that Jake wasn't even breathing hard from the exertion and the extra weight he'd been carrying.

They were in the truck and heading out of the mountains when he said, "Mel and Betty are going to be surprised at my decision to go back with you, I guess."

"They'll miss you, I'm sure."

"Who knows? Maybe I'll get them to come out for a quick visit."

When they reached the café, he pulled into the driveway and parked next to her rental car. With economical movements, he loaded his belongings as well as her things into the trunk, then took her elbow and escorted her into the café.

Betty greeted them with a beaming smile. "Well, it's good to see that storm yesterday didn't do you no harm. Why, you're up mighty bright and early. You must have gotten up with the sun."

"Just about," Jake admitted, straddling a bar stool and motioning Rebecca to sit down. "I've got a favor to ask."

Mel walked through the swinging door with two cinnamon rolls dripping with icing. Betty poured coffee and set cups in front of them. "Anything you want, Jake. You know that."

He grinned. "You haven't heard the favor."

"Doesn't matter," Mel pointed out gruffly.

Jake just shook his head. "I was wondering if I could leave my truck here with you. You'd need to drive it for me every so often, keep the battery up, that sort of thing."

Mel glanced at Rebecca before he replied. In an innocent tone he asked, "You going somewhere?"

Jake postponed answering by taking a large bite of the roll and then drinking some of the coffee. "I'm going back to Seattle with Rebecca."

"Changed your mind, did she?" Mel offered.

"Something like that."

Jake watched the older couple share a look before they each smiled at Rebecca, then gazed back at him with amusement glinting in their eyes.

Damn, but he was glad he was able to provide so much entertainment for them at his expense. Well, hell, he didn't owe them any explanations. "Will that be a problem?" he finally asked, when no one seemed inclined to say anything more.

"Not at all," Mel replied.

"Good." He glanced at Rebecca, who had demolished the roll that had been set in front of her despite a substantial breakfast at the cabin.

"You ready to go?"

She carefully wiped her mouth with a paper napkin. "Any time you are," she replied agreeably.

He finished his coffee and stood. "Then let's get this show on the road." He stepped behind the counter and gave Betty a hug. "You take care of yourself, hear? I'll stay in touch."

Mel placed his hand on Jake's shoulder. "You do that."

Once on the road they made good time to El Paso. Jake had offered to drive. He used the time to discuss his ideas about the situation at the plant. Rebecca offered some suggestions, and they reviewed the names of employees who might be more apt to have the skill and contacts to pull off a plan such as the one Jake had spotted.

By the time they boarded the plane to Seattle, they had decided on a plan of action. They lapsed into silence for some time before either one spoke again.

"Jake?" she asked.

"Umm?"

"Have you thought about where you'll stay while you're in Seattle?"

He rubbed his chin. "Not really. It isn't important. I'm sure I'll be able to find a furnished apartment close to the plant."

"I've been thinking about that, and I just want you to know that you're welcome to stay at my place, if you like." She licked her lips nervously. Before he could comment, she hurriedly continued. "The place is huge, as you know. Dad and I rattled around in it. There's plenty of room if—"

"Rebecca?"

She stopped her nervous speech and looked at him. "Yes?"

"I don't think it would be a good idea for me to stay at your place, but thanks for the offer."

"Why not? It makes sense, when you really think about it. The cook will be happy to have someone else besides me to feed. It would certainly be more convenient for you to have staff to look after your needs."

He cleared his throat. "I was thinking about you."

"What about me?"

"Your reputation."

She looked at him in surprise. "Why should you care what anyone thinks? Besides, it's nobody's business."

"No, but that won't stop them from talking. There will be all kind of speculation as it is. I don't know what Brock told them about my reasons for leaving."

"I've already told you. Dad never discussed you at all once you left, with me or anyone."

He sighed. "It will just complicate things."

"I don't see why it should."

He shook his head. "God, but you're stubborn."

"And you aren't, I suppose?"

He leaned back in his chair and closed his eyes. "All right. I'll stay at your place for a couple of days and see how things go. Once I get involved at the office, I probably won't be doing much away from the company but sleeping, anyway."

Belatedly he remembered to thank her for her offer.

"It's the least I could do, given the circumstances." She looked down at her magazine. "Don't worry. I doubt that our paths will cross at home. I manage to stay fairly busy, myself."

Good, Jake thought. *I don't need the aggravation of fighting the attraction I'm feeling. The sooner I get this mess cleared up, the faster I can return to Texas.*

For some reason the idea didn't tantalize him as much as he had hoped. Instead, he could feel himself gearing up to move once again into the cutthroat world of business. He could feel the adrenaline rush overtake him as he plotted and planned his comeback.

Rebecca watched the man beside her make notes in the files he continued to review and smiled to herself. Jake was more like her father than he would ever admit. She had understood her father quite well. The man had thrived on challenge.

Jake had met the challenge of the wilderness. Despite his retreat last year, he was returning to the business arena ready to take on whatever nasty machinations were going on. She had a hunch he'd never met a bigger challenge. She also had a hunch that he was more than man enough to handle it.

She was going to enjoy sitting ringside to watch.

Five

<hr style="width:15%">

Jake was late. He turned between the two stone pillars and followed the paved, winding driveway to the house Brock Adams had built.

There didn't seem to be enough time in each work day, even though he was generally at the office by six in the morning. Normally he never left the office before nine at night.

Tonight was different. He was expected to escort Miss Rebecca Adams to a posh party connected with some charity or other. Normally such functions weren't in his list of favorite things to do. He could just hear Mel laughing if he saw him at one of them.

However, this was one party he was glad to be able to attend, and he appreciated Rebecca's mentioning it to him last week.

Troy Wrightman was also involved with this particular charity, and Jake was extremely interested in placing himself in Mr. Wrightman's path whenever and as often as possible.

In the six weeks he'd been in Seattle, Jake had narrowed his list of possible suspects behind the problems at CPI to four men. Troy Wrightman was one of them.

Each of the four men were department heads in the company. They had worked with Brock Adams for years and therefore knew Jake.

He'd enjoyed watching their faces when he'd come in halfway through the meeting Rebecca had called the morning after she'd returned. Rebecca's comments and observations later that evening with regard to the various reactions to Jake's return had been very astute and helpful. He was grateful to have her input on the situation.

After six weeks, he was still staying with Rebecca. Since his arrival in Seattle he had never seemed to have the time to search for another place to live. She'd been right about that, as well. The house was large enough that they could go days without seeing each other, if they chose. In fact, they had to make an appointment to meet over dinner.

Most of the time the cook left Jake's meal in the refrigerator. When he got home he'd stick it in the microwave to warm before falling into bed for a few hours' sleep.

Tonight they were to eat at the party.

He left the car, one of Brock's, parked out front and took the stairs two at a time to the front door. He let himself in with the key Rebecca had given him and strode across the foyer to the curving staircase that led to the upper level.

The damn place could have easily passed for a governor's mansion with room for a few state assembly meetings. It was as impersonal as a hotel. He and Rebecca didn't even live in the same wing.

Which was just as well.

His long hours had kept him from the temptation of seeking her out to spend more time with her that was not connected with business. Due to his reasons for being there, they frequently spent time together at the office, but were rarely alone. At those times business was the only subject discussed.

His respect for her intelligence and business acumen continued to grow. Unfortunately his physical responses and reactions also continued to grow. It no longer mattered whether or not she was in his presence. Somehow Rebecca managed to haunt him and fill his thoughts despite his need for concentration.

Jake opened his bedroom door and was already undressing by the time he reached the bedside. Someone had laid out his tuxedo—freshly pressed—his pleated shirt, cummerbund, tie, socks and shoes. That would save him considerable time.

He finished stripping as he entered the bathroom and stepped into the shower, quickly soaped and rinsed himself and was out within minutes. He felt his jaw, wondering if he had time to shave. Damn, he'd have to take time. After hurriedly drying off, he quickly lathered his face and went to work on his beard.

Back in the bedroom he'd just pulled on his trousers when there was a tap on the door. He zipped them, sat down on the edge of the bed and reached for his socks as he said, "Come in."

The door opened and Rebecca peered around the door. "Are you decent?"

"A little late to ask now, don't you think? I thought you were Charles."

She stepped into the room, and Jake saw that she was ready. She wore a cream-colored satin gown that was strapless and hugged her body. Glittery jewels surrounded her neck and wrists as well as glinted among her dark curls, which she'd swept high on her head.

Jake continued pulling on his socks, determined not to look at her again if he could help it at all. Damn! Why did she have to look so good! In that one glimpse he knew he was going to be in big trouble tonight keeping his mind on his objective.

She walked toward the bed as he stood and reached for his shirt. "Are you responsible for seeing that this was all laid out for me?" he asked.

"I mentioned it to Charles. He's really invaluable, don't you think?"

"I suppose. I mean, if you're going to have a place this size, a butler is an obvious necessity."

She pushed his hand away as he attempted to attach a stud at his wrist and quickly attached it for him, making short work of it. He held out his other arm without comment, and she fastened that one, as well.

"Would you like to button my shirt, too?" he offered.

She stepped back and put her hands behind her back. "Sorry. I was just trying to help."

He turned his back to her, stuffed his shirttails into his pants and rezipped them. Then he put on his shoes and reached for the cummerbund.

"Here," he said, handing her the tie. "You might as well finish dressing me. Hope you're better at these damned things than I am."

She took the tie and draped it around his neck. He could smell her familiar scent wafting from her bare shoulders, and he forced his mind to think of other things.

"I'm glad you'll be with me tonight," she said softly. "This is the first social gathering I've attended without my father. I was really dreading going alone."

"As much as I hate to admit it, I guess I could use the break away from the office."

She grinned up at him, patting the bow in his tie and stepping back, eyeing it. "Well, I *was* thinking about offering to have a bed set up in your office so you wouldn't have to leave at all. Since Dad had already installed a shower in the bathroom, you would have had all the comforts of home."

He couldn't resist tracing his finger along her soft, creamy cheek. "I appreciate all you've done for me since I arrived," he said.

Her lashes flickered, veiling the expression in her eyes. "I'm just glad you're here," she replied softly. She reached for his jacket and held it up for him. He obligingly slipped his arms into the sleeves and tugged it over his shoulders.

She turned and headed toward the door. "We have less than fifteen minutes to get there before they begin serving dinner."

Jake self-consciously patted his tie and followed her out the door. "Aren't you going to need something on your shoulders?" he asked, following her down the stairs.

She nodded toward one of the chairs in the foyer that held a stole. He reached down and picked it up, then carefully arranged it around her shoulders. As he started to pull away he caught her eyes and recognized the vulnerability there. She'd kept such a professional demeanor around him at the office that he sometimes forgot how difficult these past several months had been for her.

He leaned down and brushed his lips over hers. "It's all going to work out just fine, 'Becca. I'll be here for as long as you need me."

Color flooded her cheeks and she stared up at him in surprise. This close he could see a darker band of gray around the iris of her silvery eyes. Those eyes had haunted more than one dream since he'd returned to the Pacific Northwest.

He took her arm and escorted her to the waiting automobile where he carefully helped her inside before getting behind the wheel and heading for their evening's entertainment.

"You look quite distinguished in your formal wear, Jake," she said as they drove down the driveway.

He gave her a brief glance from the corner of his eye. "Thanks."

"Didn't you used to attend functions of this nature when you worked with Dad?"

"Yeah."

"Didn't enjoy them any better then, huh?"

"Nope."

She laughed. He glanced at her again. She seemed relaxed. He also realized that she looked like his idea of a snooty society belle ready to dazzle everyone there. Only now he knew her much better, knew the long hours she worked each day, knew the problems she wrestled with, including the grief she felt at losing her father.

Jake reached over and took her hand, giving it a gentle squeeze. She looked at him in surprise. "Neither one of us are much like the parts we're playing tonight, are we?"

"I'm not certain I know what you mean."

"You certainly aren't some empty-headed social butterfly, and I'm no dandy, despite the pleats on my damned shirt."

She chuckled. "Thank you. I think. Is that what I look like? An empty-headed social butterfly?"

He sighed. "Guess that didn't come out exactly the way I meant it. You look beautiful and you know it. And glamorous. As though you spent all your days shopping and polishing your image."

She studied him for a moment before saying, "And you look as though you should be posing in a fashion magazine."

"The hell I do!" he growled.

He could see that she was struggling not to laugh. He grinned reluctantly and let go of her hand, saying,

"One thing for sure. You can hold your own in any situation."

She primly folded her hands in her lap and said, "Thank you, sir. I'll definitely consider that a compliment."

Several hours later the after-dinner dance was in full swing, and Jake stepped onto the terrace that extended the ballroom out into the open air. The night air had kept most people inside but the French doors opening onto the terrace were all open.

He leaned against the wall and took a deep breath, glad to take a break. As far as he was concerned the evening had been a success. Troy Wrightman had seemed unnerved when he'd seen the two of them walk in together.

No one at the office knew that Jake was staying at the Adams residence. It must have come as a shock for Troy to think that Jake and Rebecca might be seeing each other on a social basis. If he was the one Jake was looking for, it would make sense that he wouldn't want Jake to take too much interest in Rebecca's affairs.

When Rebecca had announced Jake's return to the company, she had made it sound perfectly plausible that the man her father had spent years training to run the company would be the logical one to step into his shoes now that he was gone.

Two women stepped through one of the nearby doorways and walked to the balustrade. Hoping they wouldn't stay long, Jake lingered in the darker shadows near the wall of the building and waited for the cool air to force them back inside.

They seemed to be in the middle of a gossip session.

"Did you notice the look on her face while they were dancing?" said one. "She looked like the cat who swallowed the canary. It's a wonder there weren't yellow feathers dripping from her mouth."

Jake frowned at the comment. Speaking of someone being catty!

"And the way she follows him with her eyes whenever she thinks he isn't watching," said the other. "It's almost laughable. It's obvious she's hoping her daddy's money is going to buy this one for her!"

"It really is sad, isn't it," the first one said, without a hint of sadness, "how hard Rebecca has tried all these years to get a man's attention."

Jake stiffened when he heard Rebecca's name. Surely they weren't talking about Rebecca Adams.

"I know," the other one replied. "She always hung on Brock's arm like a leech in an effort to get him to notice her at these affairs. Not even her own father paid her any attention!"

Damn! Rebecca *was* the topic of their vicious remarks, and there wasn't a hell of a lot he could do about it. If they'd been men, he would have definitely interrupted their attack, but taking a swing at a couple of pseudo-ladies would not be the most politic thing to do. Instead, he was a captive audience of one unless he wanted to risk giving his presence away.

"Well, you must admit that she has excellent taste in men. Did you see the shoulders on him?"

Oh, great. Jake leaned his head against the wall and closed his eyes in resignation. Wasn't it bad enough that he was forced to listen to comments about Rebecca without throwing him in there as well?

"And did you see the way she was dancing with him? It was a wonder the poor man could draw breath, the way she plastered herself against him."

"Did you get his name?"

"No, but he couldn't be from around here or I'd certainly recognize him."

"Maybe he works for her father's company."

"Well, whoever he is, he isn't part of our set, or I would have seen him at the club, either playing tennis or golf or at the pool. With a build like that, I'd dearly love to see him stripped!"

"Oh, Amanda!" the other said, giggling. "You're just awful!"

"Let's go back inside, shall we? It's much cooler out here than I expected."

Jake watched them drift back inside, still whispering and giggling to each other. Now those two reminded him of the kind of women he'd known at college—spoiled and pampered, thinking they could have whatever their hearts desired.

He'd been the target of some of their desires and knew from painful experience what it was like to get caught up in one of their games.

He was ashamed that he'd thought Rebecca was just like them. All those years he'd worked with Brock, when he'd turned down dinner invitations to Brock's home with feeble excuses, when he'd distanced himself from Brock's daughter whenever possible, he had thought she was a shallow, immature brat. He was just as guilty as those two for not seeing Rebecca for who she was.

After a few minutes he stepped back into the ballroom and looked around for Rebecca. He spotted her about halfway across the room, her back to him. He recognized her straight posture, the way she held her head, the sparkle of the jewels in her hair. Perhaps she would be ready to leave shortly. He knew he was fed up with the place. She was talking to a couple of—

Dear God, the two women standing there talking so animatedly with her were the same two who had been out on the terrace a few minutes before. Both women were acting overly sweet to her, as though she were a dear friend, when only moments earlier they had been making cruel remarks about her. How could they think that Rebecca couldn't attract any man she wanted! Why, she had more class in her tiniest toenail than both those biddies put together!

Since her back was to the door and his approach, the two women spotted him before Rebecca knew he was behind her. He noticed that one elbowed the other and both of them wore sly grins. What were they hoping for now, more grist for their gossip mill?

Well, maybe he'd give it to them.

When he reached Rebecca he slipped his arms around her, wrapping them firmly around her waist, and pulled her against his chest. She gave a start that he controlled by the grip he had on her, then he nudged her head aside by placing a kiss on her neck and whispering, "Just play along," under his breath.

He felt her relax slightly against him, but her breathing was far from even. "Oh, hi, Jake," she said a little shakily. "We were just talking about you."

I'll just bet you were. "Mmm," he murmured against her neck. "Were you?"

She quivered and tried to turn in his arms, but he merely tightened his hold. "Uh, mmm, yes. Amanda and Millicent happened to mention that they hadn't been introduced to you."

Slowly he raised his head from where he'd been nuzzling Rebecca's earlobe. He gave each of them a steady look that revealed nothing of his thoughts. Both women wore ridiculously eager smiles.

"Jake, I'd like you to meet Millicent Trusdale and Amanda Wrightman. This is Jake Taggart. He's president of CPI Industries."

"Wrightman?" he repeated slowly. "Any relation to Troy Wrightman?"

Amanda nodded eagerly. "That's my father. I had no idea you and Daddy worked together. I can't imagine how it happened that we never met before," she gushed.

Still holding Rebecca pressed against him, he said, "I don't do much socializing. When I'm not working, I like to spend all my spare time with 'Becca." He dropped his voice. "Don't I, darling?"

She gave an infinitesimal jerk at the endearment.

Having her pressed so intimately against him was also causing a definite reaction in him over which he had no control. He shifted slightly so that only one of his arms was wrapped around her. He kept her close to his side.

"Why, Rebecca," Millicent squealed. "How could you have kept this wonderful man all to yourself? Just how long has this been going on?" she asked archly.

Before she could respond, Jake drawled, "Oh, I joined the company almost six years ago." He gave Rebecca a melting look. "From the time I first laid eyes on Rebecca I let everyone around know that she was private stock."

All three women stared at him with varying degrees of shock and surprise. In fact, Rebecca's jaw had just dropped. Afraid that the other two women would recognize the amazement in her expression for what it was, he hastily leaned down and covered her mouth with his...and promptly forgot the purpose of the kiss when his lips touched hers.

Her mouth was soft, moist and slightly open, an invitation he couldn't resist. Turning her more fully toward him, he slipped his tongue between her lips, quickly discovering that he wanted much more than a mere taste.

Forcing himself to remember their audience, he reluctantly pulled far enough away to whisper, "Are you ready to go yet, Sweetheart? I'm tired of sharing you with all these people."

Rebecca could only nod, her eyes wide.

He turned to the other two who stood with mouths agape—not nearly so attractively as Rebecca—and said, "It was a pleasure meeting you, ladies. I hope you'll excuse us. Sometimes it's hard to remember to be a gentleman. There are times when I have a tremendous urge to toss her over my shoulder and haul her off to the nearest cave."

He nodded and, with his arm still around her waist, guided Rebecca out to the hallway where he retrieved her wrap, then led her to where he'd parked the car.

"What in the world was that all about?" she finally asked in a faint voice once they were both inside the car.

"How well do you know those two?"

She blinked. "Amanda and Millicent?"

He nodded.

"Well, I guess I've always known them. I mean, we went through school together, although I went back East to college and they stayed here. We've been friends for years."

He leaned toward her, sliding his arm around her shoulders. "Then I suggest you find a higher caliber of friends!" His kiss immediately took over where the other one had ended so precipitously.

This time he took a leisurely approach to exploring the delicious taste and contour of her lips, teeth and mouth, lazily nipping at her bottom lip, then sucking on it in a soothing gesture. He cupped his hand at the nape of her neck, losing himself in the moment of discovery.

Eventually he had to pause for air. With a great deal of reluctance he raised his head and stared down at the woman in his arms.

She was struggling to get air in her lungs. His breathing wasn't too even, either. He enjoyed watching the quick rise and fall of her delectable breasts as she tried to calm her breathing.

"How much...have you had...to drink tonight?" she managed to ask.

"No more than you. You've been with me all evening."

"We only had wine for dinner. We both switched to tonic water when the dancing began."

"Exactly."

"But then—I mean— Why were you so—so—"

"Amorous?"

"Is that what that was?"

"You mean you didn't recognize it?" he asked, with just a slight hint of hurt in his voice.

She stared at him for a long moment before she hesitantly said, "I've never seen you behave like this before."

He straightened in his seat and started the car. "I hate catty women." He pulled out of the parking place and started home.

"Are you talking about Amanda and Millicent?"

"Among others. I just don't see the point of women having to talk about each other in slighting terms."

"But they weren't saying anything slighting! In fact, they were asking all kinds of questions about you when you walked up."

"So I decided to become the mystery man in your life. Do you mind?"

She looked at him askance. "Why should I need a mystery man in my life?"

"For a little romance and adventure, perhaps?"

"Are you on drugs?"

"Damn it, Rebecca. Here I try to be a little romantic and you start accusing me of stuff!"

"All right, Jake, all right. There's no reason to get excited."

"And you don't need to use that soothing tone of voice on me as though I just escaped from the state asylum."

She was quiet, and when he risked a glance at her he saw her carefully watching the way he was driving. Damn. She really *did* think he'd slipped a cog somewhere.

"All right. So maybe I did act a little out of character."

"A little?"

"I acted on impulse, okay?"

She cleared her throat. "Do you get these impulses often?"

She sounded so prim that he couldn't help smiling. He darted another glance at her. "Obviously not often enough, but if I offended you, I'm sorry."

"Oh, you didn't, uh, offend me. I mean, not really, uh, exactly. I think *surprised* is the better word. Or maybe *shocked—astounded—flabbergasted—*"

"I get the point, 'Becca, although I don't see why it should have been *that* big a shock. After all, you're a very attractive woman and I'm a very normal—"

"I am?" She coughed. "I mean, you find me attractive?"

He turned into the driveway and drove past the house to the garage without answering. Only then did he realize the trap he'd unsuspectingly laid for himself. And *he* had done it, that's for sure. Nobody else.

He helped her out of the car and walked her to the back entrance of the house, through the back rooms to the foyer and paused at the bottom of the winding steps.

Taking her face between his hands he looked down at her. There was so much innocence in that face. So much trust. How dare those women make snide remarks about her lack of a social life. It wasn't because she wasn't attractive. She'd been trying too hard to prove something to her father.

No wonder Brock had hoped he would show some interest in her. She'd be a hell of a lot better off with him than some bozo who would—

Whoa! Wait a minute. What was he thinking of here? He didn't have any intention of getting involved with anyone—not even Rebecca. Especially not 'Becca.

He'd been hired to do a job, then he was going back to the mountains where he belonged. What Rebecca chose to do with her life was up to her. Whatever anyone wanted to say about her had absolutely nothing to do with him.

Maybe that damned dinner wine was more potent than he thought, after all!

"Jake? What is it? Why are you looking at me like that?"

"Like what?" he murmured, stroking her cheek with his finger.

"I don't know. As though you can't decide whether or not you want to kiss me again."

"Oh, there's no question but that I want to kiss you again. The battle is whether I dare."

She smiled, her eyes shining. "I've never seen you in this mood before."

"That's not surprising. I don't think I've ever been in this mood before."

She went up on her toes and kissed him, sliding her hands slowly over his chest and up into his hair. He forced himself not to move. When she eased away from him, she said, "I miss your long hair. I think that was the real you—that man I met from the mountains."

"Not very civilized, I'm afraid, despite the costume." He glanced down at his clothes but somehow couldn't let go of her. His hands continued to cup her face, his fingers toying with her earlobes, a curl, smoothing her eyebrow.

"Is something the matter?" she finally asked.

He forced himself to drop his hands and step away. "Nothing major. I've probably been putting in too many hours at work. Maybe I'll take a couple of days off."

She nodded. "Good idea. You certainly have earned them."

He made a wide circle around her and started up the stairs. "Well, guess we should both get to bed—I mean, get some rest. Good night."

She waited until he reached the landing before she said, "Jake?"

He looked down at where she stood under the massive chandelier, the light catching the sparkle of jewels all around her. From here she looked like a fairytale princess. What he had to remember was that he was not the prince.

"Yes, 'Becca?"

"Do you think you found out anything by going with me tonight?"

"Oh, yeah." *More than I ever wanted to know.* "We'll talk about it at the office on Monday. See you later."

It was one of the hardest things he'd had to do in recent years, to turn around and walk away from the woman looking up at him so trustingly.

The lights of downtown Seattle decorated the skyline outside his office windows, when Jake finally shoved back from his desk and stood, stretching to get the kinks out of his back.

Despite spring's rapid approach, darkness continued to fall long before he was finished with each day's work. Where had the time gone?

He glanced at his watch. He'd been at the office for fourteen hours. Long enough day for anyone. It would feel good to return to the house, which had come to be a haven to him in many ways. There was something to be said for a smooth-running home life where meals awaited him, clothes were always clean, neatly pressed and put away, and a sweetheart of a woman resided.

In the weeks since he'd escorted Rebecca to the charity ball, he'd had plenty of time to face what had been happening to him. He didn't like it. Not at all.

Jake had always known how he'd intended to conduct his life. He'd learned early on not to allow anyone past his defenses. Mel and Betty had always been a part of his life but even they respected the boundaries he'd set around himself. At least, most of the time.

Now he felt betrayed by his own feelings for someone.

Wouldn't ol' Brock be laughing his head off if he only knew that Jake had fallen head over heels for Brock's daughter?

There was a certain amount of irony in that, he had to admit. A few years ago it would have worked out just fine. He had intended to run the company on a permanent basis, so what would have been more convenient than to have fallen in love with the boss's daughter?

Only now she was the boss, and he had no intention of being a part of the company much longer.

Within a few weeks, if everything went as he planned, he would have enough hard evidence to be able to expose Troy Wrightman, have him arrested and turn the company back over to Rebecca.

He'd told her that was what he was going to do. He was in the process of doing it. Then he was heading back to Texas.

However, he knew these few months had changed him so that nothing would ever be quite the same for him. Not that he had any intention of letting her know how he felt. No, he intended to retreat again into the mountains where he was safe from the pain of emotional attachments.

If he hadn't been in such a blasted fury over the remarks made by those stupid women, he wouldn't be in the fix he was in right now. In his effort to protect Rebecca from possible hurt, he'd thrown himself into a situation that had blown up in his face.

He'd kissed her, and he'd held her, and he'd discovered the woman who had the ability to hurt him because of the way he felt about her. He'd never felt so vulnerable. Not since he was a kid. And he hated the feeling.

Since that night he'd avoided being alone with her, which wasn't really difficult. They'd rarely seen each other away from the office, anyway.

He'd spent the weekend after the ball riding the ferries among the San Juan Islands. He'd spent the night at a bed and breakfast, spent the evening in a local bar and toyed with the idea of encouraging one of the women there who'd shown a decided interest in him.

The problem had been that she was the wrong woman.

That's when he'd known he was in deep trouble.

Since that time he'd established a routine of working long hours, returning home late at night and swimming in the indoor heated pool until he was exhausted enough to sleep. Most nights he dreamed restlessly until it was time to get up and go back to the office.

Only a few more weeks, now, and he could leave. He was determined to get through them without letting anyone know, especially Rebecca, how hard he'd fallen for her.

Rebecca had a secret vice. One she had never shared with anyone. Of course her parents knew she liked to paint. After all, they had paid for art lessons. However, they had also paid for tennis lessons, dancing lessons, music lessons, ballet lessons and horseback riding lessons.

What Rebecca had never shared with anyone was the subject matter that captivated her, that soothed her spirit and calmed her soul. What absorbed her attention when she wasn't working, eating or sleeping was painting underwater fantasies. She currently had over twenty large canvases—safely under lock and key—denoting an entire world that existed in a wonderland of her creative mind.

The alarming bit of information that she had just discovered as she cleaned her brushes late one evening was that for the past several weeks the mermen she was adding to the groupings of mermaids, seahorses pulling a giant clam shell, colorful castles and iridescent crystals, all looked like Jake Taggart.

The shock of recognition had her staring at her latest canvas. There was no mistaking those eyes—or the wide shoulders and muscular chest. She'd only seen Jake without a shirt once or twice, but obviously those glimpses had been memorable enough glimpses to have stimulated her subconscious.

"Well, what do you know," she murmured to herself while she studied the painting in front of her. It wasn't difficult to trace back when her subconscious had taken over.

Ever since the night of the charity ball when Jake had behaved so out of character, he'd been haunting her thoughts, both day and night.

She'd never been able to understand his strange behavior. When they'd returned to work the following Monday he'd been his usual, formal self, the epitome of the professional executive. Not by so much as a hint of a glance, expression, or body language did he appear to remember what had taken place between them.

And what, after all, had happened, really? He had kissed her, that's all. She'd been the one who'd felt all of those fabled things that were supposed to happen when that one particular person—that dream lover, that soul mate—finally came upon the scene. Like an impressionable adolescent, she'd definitely succumbed to the man's considerable charms.

She felt like Sleeping Beauty, unawakened until her prince had come along. Oh, boy! And had he awakened her. It was all she could do to behave in the usual manner at the office. As soon as he walked into a room her heart started drumming loud enough to be heard by everyone there.

Whenever he spoke she found herself watching his mouth, remembering how it had felt pressed against hers, nibbling, soothing, possessing her. She felt as though he'd laid claim to her. Hadn't he mentioned something about carrying her to his cave? Yes. That's the way she'd felt.

And then he'd just walked away from her. Since then he'd acted as though nothing at all had happened between them. Business as usual.

So now she was painting him into her fantasies, making him a part of her life in the only way she knew how while he was probably counting the days until he could return to Texas.

She found the thought depressing.

She thoughtfully studied her work. It was no wonder she didn't want anyone to know about her paintings. They revealed too much about her.

Her paintings reflected her inner yearning for a sparkling, magical world filled with friendly water-dwelling sprites. Her mother might have smiled and labeled them whimsical. Her father would have snorted and waved them away.

Her romantic nature was firmly locked away with her paintings, to be brought out only when she was assured of her privacy.

Now here she was staring at the results of her wildly romantic imaginings. She'd laugh if she wasn't so dismayed. Jake Taggart? The lone wolf of West Texas? The mysterious mountain man?

No. This wouldn't do. Absolutely not. She wasn't ready for this. She would never be ready for this, not with somebody like Jake. Oh, she intended to marry someday. She wanted a husband, a family. But she had very definite ideas about the kind of man she knew would make her happy.

Jake Taggart didn't fit any of her ideas.

The only thing Jake Taggart did was make her toes curl and her heart race.

She certainly didn't intend to do anything about it. Did she?

Would it be so wrong to explore all these new feelings that he'd awakened in her? Just because Jake wasn't marriage material didn't mean she couldn't enjoy him while he was here, did it?

She'd been so busy all these years, getting her education and working to prove to her father that she could do the job she'd been hired to do, that she had allowed her social life to lapse into a terminal coma.

Most of her school friends were married, at least once. A few had begun their families.

She, on the other hand, couldn't remember the last time she'd been out on a date. Her father had been her escort at civic functions, just as she'd provided hostess duties whenever he'd done any business entertaining. Since his death she'd had no energy or inclination to accept any of the invitations to the various organizations they had supported in the past. Instead, she had sent a check along with her apologies and continued to deal with the daily running of the company.

Until the night of the charity ball.

The question was, what did she intend to do about all these feelings Jake Taggart had stirred up?

She found the question provocative in and of itself. Instead of passively accepting the status quo, she could actually choose some course of action that might change it.

An interesting thought. An empowering thought.

Her reputation was safe, if that had been one of her concerns. Since several members of the permanent staff lived on the premises it couldn't be said that she and Jake were alone in any sense of the word.

What they had, however, and what she hadn't appreciated until now, was privacy. The staff retired to the third floor each evening.

She glanced at her watch and wondered if Jake was home. It was after eleven. Surely he'd be home by now. She'd had dinner early tonight and retired to the study off her bedroom to paint. If Jake was home and if he hadn't already gone to bed, where might she find him?

He rarely used her father's study downstairs. Once or twice she'd seen him in the game room shooting billiards. And, of course, there was the evening she'd seen him at the swimming pool.

She smiled to herself. The swimming pool. Even if he wasn't there, she would certainly enjoy taking a few laps in the pool to work some of the kinks out of her neck and shoulders after the hours she'd spent at the easel.

Rebecca felt a tingle of anticipation while she dug through her store of swimsuits and found the one she'd bought in France the last time she and her father had visited there. She'd never shown it to her father. To be perfectly honest, she'd never worn it at all, but she had liked the idea of owning something so decidedly impractical and unlike her businesslike image.

The thong bikini bottom left very little to the imagination while the top barely covered the rosy tips of her breasts. She stood in front of the bathroom mirror and inspected her body. All those salads she'd been eating most evenings had obviously done their job. There were no obvious bulges showing. There was nothing she could do about her too small breasts or her too slender legs, but all in all, she didn't look so bad.

The question was, could she actually take the chance of running into Jake at the swimming pool wearing something so revealing?

The smile she gave her image was slow and uncharacteristically seductive. *You bet,* she muttered to herself.

She found her beach jacket that demurely concealed her unclad body, slipped on a pair of sandals and went downstairs.

The house was quiet and mostly dark. Only the sconces in the foyer were left burning all night, giving necessary light to the staircase.

She went through the back of the house into the glass-walled addition her father had built to enclose the pool for their year-round enjoyment.

The water in the pool was so still it looked like painted glass in the silvery moonlight. No one was there. She felt a twinge of disappointment before shrugging it off. What had she expected, anyway? Perhaps these long hours painting her underwater world had warped her brain and she was trying to live out some of those fantasies!

With a chuckle, she slid the beach jacket off her shoulders and stepped into the pool, following the steps down through the shallow end until she was deep enough to swim.

The water felt like warm silk, sensuously wrapping around her body, and she sighed, pleased that she had thought of this wonderfully relaxing way to finish the evening. She didn't take advantage of the convenience of having the pool nearly enough. It was so easy to fall into a routine and forget some of the pleasures that life offered.

She rolled over onto her back and closed her eyes, drifting in the caressing slickness of the liquid, her thoughts returning to Jake and how his likeness continued to crop up in her imaginings and fantasies.

Jake sat in the hot tub in the corner of the room wondering how in the hell he'd managed to get himself in this situation.

Only once in all the weeks he'd been here had he ever seen Rebecca at the pool, and that had been early one evening. She had never come downstairs this late at night...which is why he happened to be sitting in the hot tub without his bathing suit.

Instead of going to his room first, he'd come in, stripped out of his clothes and crawled into the bubbling massage of water, effectively working on his tired muscles. He hadn't even bothered to check the kitchen to see what had been left for him to eat.

So now what did he do?

The tub was in the shadows at the end of the room. There was a better-than-even chance she wouldn't see him if he chose to remain quiet. On the other hand, what could he say if she discovered his presence and asked why he hadn't said something when she first came in?

Good question.

The problem was he hadn't seen her come in. He'd been resting his head on the side of the tub with his eyes closed when he'd sensed that he wasn't alone. He hadn't heard her, which wasn't surprising with the low hum of the water pump drowning out most of the night noises.

He'd opened his eyes in time to see her remove a short jacket that revealed she was wearing very little more than he was. He hadn't seen anything but her back before she went into the water, but from that angle, her swimming attire appeared to be no more than a couple of shoestrings.

He watched her swim up and down the pool a few laps before she rolled over onto her back. Even in the shadowy moonlight he realized that what she wore hadn't been designed to conceal anything from view.

He closed his eyes and mentally cursed his stupidity. Too bad he'd gotten used to having the house to himself whenever he'd arrived home this late at night. He'd known she was there, somewhere, but had never turned toward the wing where she slept, when he'd climbed the stairs.

So now what do you do? he asked himself.

Since he'd intended to swim after his dip into the hot tub, he wondered how much he would reveal if he decided to slip into the pool while she was still there. It was dark; how much could she see?

Or should he say something first? And have her spot him. Then she'd ask why he had continued to sit in the tub without calling attention to himself.

Nothing had trained him for the correct etiquette in this particular situation.

Maybe she would be leaving soon. Maybe, if he just waited her out, he'd be able to—to—

His unexpected sneeze eliminated his need to choose the best way out of his dilemma.

Six

Jake groaned as he heard the sudden splashing in the pool that verified Rebecca now knew she was not alone.

"Jake?" she asked, her voice sounding shaky.

"Yeah, it's me, 'Becca. Sorry. I didn't mean to scare you."

She swam toward the steps and climbed out of the pool, padding toward him. The moonlight created stripes of light across the floor, which she walked through as she came toward him—first revealing, then concealing her from his view. However, there was sufficient light for him to see that she obviously hadn't dressed for an audience.

You certainly couldn't tell from her demeanor.

"I didn't know you were here," she said nonchalantly, for all the world as though they'd just met at the breakfast table, dressed for the office. She paused beside the pool and trailed her fingers through the roiling water. "Oh, this feels great. May I join you?"

"Be my guest," he replied dryly. "However, I might as well tell you now that I neglected to put on my swimming trunks. I didn't expect to see anybody down here at this time of night."

All the while he was making his explanation he watched as she crawled into the tub and settled across from him with a pleasurable sigh, ignoring his warning. "Oh, yes, I can see why you'd head straight to this after a long day. Doesn't it feel great?" She waited for him to reply, and when he didn't say anything, she eyed him a little uncertainly. "I hope my joining you hasn't caused you any embarrassment."

He shrugged. "I was thinking along similar lines where you were concerned. I guess we're both adults, here. It isn't as though we haven't seen bare bodies before." Which was a good thing, he added to himself, since she might as well be nude.

She grinned, wearing a mischievous look that was totally unfamiliar to him. He found it adorable. "You credit me with a little more sophistication than I deserve, I'm afraid," she confided cheerfully. "Except for photographs, statues and other works of art, I've never seen an adult male nude before. Are you offering to assist me in my continuing education?"

He almost choked. "Of course not!" he said in a strangled voice.

Damned if she didn't look disappointed!

"You're kidding me, of course," he said after a moment.

"Nope."

Now why did the idea of her virginal status seem to send shock waves through his system? The news should mean nothing to him. Nothing at all.

"Why not?" he heard himself ask.

"Why not what?"

He cleared his throat. "I mean, why haven't you seen an adult male stripped to the buff before?"

She shrugged. "Guess I've never been that interested ... or maybe it's because I've been too busy pursuing my goals." She sighed. "With the schedule I've been keeping for most of my life, I haven't had many opportunities."

Her foot accidentally brushed against his calf. Instead of jerking it away, she gently rubbed her toes down the length of his leg to his ankle, then she reversed the movement and slowly traced his leg with her foot back up to his knee.

An electrified cattle prod couldn't have jolted him more. What the hell did she think she was doing? He shifted, deliberately giving her more space in the tub.

Her comments about the lack of a social life unfortunately reminded him of the conversation he'd overheard at the charity ball. He'd been an idiot that night, making the near-fatal—at least to his peace of mind— mistake of believing she'd needed protection from other people's opinions.

Why hadn't he minded his own business? He'd always been good at that. Why hadn't he just—

"Jake?" Her voice sounded soft and dreamy in the stillness of the cavernous room.

"Yeah?" he replied after a moment.

"Are you sorry you came back to CPI?"

He let go of the air he'd inadvertently stored in his lungs. Taking another deep breath he forced himself to relax slightly before responding. "No. Not at all."

"I'm glad. I wouldn't want you to be unhappy here."

"I'm fine."

"You don't seem to have any friends in Seattle. Don't you miss them?"

He didn't answer right away. Rebecca didn't mind. Just being there with him was much more than she'd ever expected to have happen. So when he finally spoke she wasn't certain that she heard him correctly. What she thought he said was "I've never had a friend."

Surely she was mistaken in what she'd heard. After another long pause, she murmured, "Not ever?"

"Not really."

"Not even a school friend?"

"Especially then. I was too busy working. I didn't want Mel and Betty using up their retirement fund to help me through school. Besides, I've always been something of a loner."

She laughed. She couldn't help it. "Really! I wouldn't have guessed."

"I've never been good in social situations."

"Now that's where you could have fooled me. I remember watching you and Dad work a room during some of the business functions I attended over the years. Talk about a couple of pros!"

"That was different. I knew what was expected of me in a business situation. I knew what to say. I don't understand friendships." He thought back to Amanda and Millicent. If their examples of friendship were typical, he knew damned well he didn't want any part of it.

Rebecca pulled her knees to her chest and wrapped her arms around her legs. "I'd like to be your friend, Jake," she said softly. "But you'll have to help me."

"In what way?" he asked cautiously.

"Talk to me."

He frowned. "I thought that's what we were doing."

She rested her chin on her knees. "Yes, that's true. And it's a start. The thing about friendships is that you share something about yourself with the other person. Something special. It's like a gift you offer. Hopefully, the person will share something in return."

He gave her a steady look. "Are you serious?"

She held his gaze. "Absolutely. Inviting me to see your home in the mountains could be construed as an overture of friendship. Showing me your valley and the wildlife—all of that was allowing me a glimpse of your private self, who you really are. As a result of that trip I opened my home to you...another offer of friendship."

"You just wanted me to come back to Seattle, as I recall."

"True. I wanted the man who had trained with my father to bring his experiences and his knowledge of the company into play in order to salvage what we could. However, it was the man who lived alone in a hidden mountain retreat that has intrigued me and caused me to want to learn more about him."

"Why?"

"I dunno, exactly. I guess it's the two distinctly different aspects of who you are that I find so unusual. In the business world you exude confidence and an urbane polish that suggests a privileged background. And yet, from what you have told me, you've spent much of your life in the wilderness, learning survival at the most primitive level."

"And you find that unusual?"

"Very."

Without warning he reached for her and with a strong tug on her wrist pulled her across the tub toward him. "I've decided I'd like to be your friend," he said with a half smile. He guided her so that she was lying across his thighs, her hands resting against his chest.

The unexpected move caught her unprepared and left her breathless. With a nervous chuckle she attempted to sit up by pressing her palms against his chest. Her fingers slid across the smooth and muscled surface. She was very aware that she was sitting on bare thighs.

He straightened slightly and placed a kiss on her cheek, another one on the tip of her nose and a third one on her slightly opened mouth.

With a tiny groan she lifted her arms around his neck and leaned against him, returning the slight pressure of his kiss and deepening it.

Jake quickly realized that he'd made a strategical error. In his impulsive effort to distract her from her subject of conversation—himself—he had momentarily forgotten that the situation was fraught with complications, the most acute being the fact that they were very much alone, unclothed and, at the moment, Rebecca's behavior was uninhibited, which wasn't helping his restraint in the least.

And yet, wasn't this what his dreams had been full of during the past several weeks—holding her, kissing her, making love to her?

Had he lost his mind?

The thought drifted through him as though it had been suggested by someone else. He ignored it. She was already settling into his lap as though there was nowhere else that she would rather be. Her response to his move was all the encouragement he needed to wrap his arms around her and to thoroughly explore once again the delectable shape and texture of her eager mouth.

For the moment he would allow himself the simple pleasure of enjoying the situation.

Rebecca tightened her arms around his neck, afraid he might pull away from her before she had the chance to experience once again those wonderful, tingling sensations that occurred when he kissed her. Who knew when she might be able to kiss Jake again? She wanted to luxuriate in this golden opportunity to live out some of her fantasies.

Her breasts were pressed tightly against his chest. She shifted slightly, wanting to feel the rough texture of the curls against her skin. The minuscule covering across her chest was hopelessly inadequate. The flimsy material had shifted so that her bare breasts were now pressed against him.

Jake curled his fingers around one of them and gently stroked the soft roundness that filled his hand. What the hell was he doing? He had to stop this right now before—

But it was too late to stop Rebecca's suddenly urgent need to resolve so many questions that had gone unanswered throughout her life. She wanted to discover what all these delicious feelings meant, where they led, and she wanted Jake Taggart to be her teacher.

The buoyancy of the water aided her movement as she turned more fully toward him, straddling his thighs. She felt his body's reaction to her. Instead of being dismayed and pulling back, she made a pleased sound deep in her throat and touched him.

"'Becca—!" Jake whispered in a strangled voice.

"Mmm?" Her fingers continued to explore the length and breadth of him. She eased closer, drawing him ever nearer.

"You don't know— This really isn't a very good— Oh, 'Becca. . . ." His voice faded into a groan as she positioned her body over his hardened length and slowly lowered herself onto him.

She couldn't believe the indescribable sensations rippling through her. Her mind had shut down and her instincts had taken over. There was an uncomfortable moment when she discovered that her heightened senses couldn't disguise the pain of joining with a man for the first time. She stiffened, her eyes widening, and Jake gathered her close, holding her in his arms without moving. The pain eased as her body adjusted to the new sensations.

Jake began to kiss her once again, the tenderness of his touch causing her to melt into his embrace.

In time she wanted more than gentleness. She wasn't exactly sure what it was she wanted, but she knew there was something she was striving for that would—

She began to move her hips. Jake guided her, urging her on. She couldn't believe how good it felt to be with him like this. After picking up her pace to increase the pleasure, she experienced a silent explosion somewhere deep inside, as her body clenched around him, then quivered into wave after wave of release. With a groan, Jake followed her lead, and they continued to cling to each other in the soothing aftermath of their coming together.

For a long time the only movement was the bubbling water around them. Eventually Jake muttered, "It's a wonder we didn't drown ourselves in this thing."

Rebecca wondered if she would ever have the energy to move or whether she could continue to drape herself around him forever. He stood, still holding her in his arms, and stepped out of the tub. He placed her on one of the benches nearby, then went over to where she had left her robe beside the pool.

She couldn't take her eyes off his lithe, naked form, so beautiful in its clean, sculpted lines as he moved between light and shadow. He appeared comfortable in his unclothed state, as though he were alone. Rebecca glanced down and realized that she still wore the scraps of her bikini and quickly adjusted them before he turned around. How strange that she should gain some comfort by wearing such an ineffective item of clothing.

Jake returned to where she sat, carrying her robe. She stood, her knees still wobbling, and he put the robe around her. "We stayed in there too long."

She glanced up at him, but his expression was unreadable. He was right, of course. The body shouldn't be submerged in too-warm water for more than a few minutes at a time. But she had a hunch he wasn't referring to the temperature of the water.

Her eyes met his. "There's no harm done." Her gaze remained steady despite her nervousness.

"You think not?"

She couldn't read anything from his expression or his tone of voice. It was up to her to carry them through this awkward situation.

"We're both adults, Jake. Let's don't make any more of this than it is."

"Okay. You tell me, then. Just what is this?"

She lifted her shoulders in a tiny shrug. "The mood of the moment, perhaps?"

He didn't say anything for a long time. "I find it interesting that this particular 'mood of the moment' never struck you before, as you mentioned earlier." His voice dropped. "Why me? Why now?"

She studied him for a long moment of silence before saying, "You've turned back into the rational businessman once again with your need for answers. Isn't it enough that we spent some pleasant time together? Do we need to analyze it?"

"You tell me. After all, you're the boss here."

Her face flamed. She felt as though he'd slapped her. "So what does that make you, some sex slave, here to do my bidding?"

After another long moment of silence, he chuckled. "Now there's a thought! Sex slave, huh?" He shook his head, looking away from her.

"Would you mind putting something on?" she finally said, having trouble fighting the urge to stare at his body, to touch it, to ask him to hold her for a while longer.

"Sorry, milady. I didn't mean to offend your sensibilities." He reached for a towel and lazily wrapped it around his middle.

There was no way she was going to be able to win a verbal duel with this man. She was way over her head, and she knew it. As soon as he turned away, she spun around and hurried to the door. She was going to have to deal with her reactions to what had happened in the privacy of her room. Maybe she would be able to face him better tomorrow.

Right now all she wanted was to be alone.

Rebecca reached the refuge of her room with a sense of relief. She'd managed to escape Jake's presence without humiliating herself further.

She could scarcely believe her actions. She had thrown herself at the man, practically begged him to make love to her. He'd obliged her, of course. She shivered and realized she was leaning against the door as though there was a possibility he might seek her out.

Fat chance. He was probably laughing his fool head off at her behavior. She headed toward the shower, shedding her swimsuit cover and bikini on the way. She wasn't at all sure she wanted to question her motives for seeking him out.

Hadn't she accomplished exactly what she'd set out to do? But somehow in her fantasies she'd pictured herself as the one in control. When they'd discussed friendship she'd thought that she could help him in some way. Instead he'd taken charge and sought to teach her a few things.

She wasn't sorry to have experienced lovemaking with Jake. It had been so much more than just curiosity, but what had happened hadn't prepared her for how she would feel afterward.

Only now did she face the fact that she had wanted him to want her. She had hoped that he would feel a new bond with her as a result of their joining.

Instead he had taken what she'd offered him, then had had the nerve to remind her that since she was his technical boss, he hadn't been given much choice in the matter.

By the time she stepped out of the shower and finished drying her hair, Rebecca knew that she had made a grave tactical error. From now on she would have to walk a thin line with Jake or he might leave the company before he'd resolved all the difficulties.

She would have to impose a strict restraint upon herself in order not to allow him to see just how vulnerable she was where he was concerned.

* * *

Jake watched her march away from him, her back impossibly stiff. For the first time in a very long time, he hated himself. He'd been so set on protecting himself that he had hurt her. Badly.

Damn it. Hadn't she known that she was playing with fire, despite all the water around? It was a wonder the hot tub hadn't been reduced to steam when she'd crawled in there with him.

But there had been no reason to hurt her. He cringed when he thought of some of the things he'd said, as though what had happened between them hadn't mattered to him, one way or the other.

Hadn't she said the same thing, though? Hadn't she been using him in an attempt to gain some experience?

Damn those women, anyway. He certainly hadn't pitied Rebecca her innocent state. He felt like a heel for so freely taking what she'd offered, regardless of her reasons.

She'd felt so good in his arms. As soon as he'd taken her out of the tub he'd wanted her again. If he was her only experience of a male nude in living flesh, then she was bound to have gotten the idea that all men walked around with a portion of their anatomy imitating a flag pole!

He scrubbed his face with his hand, knowing what he was going to have to do. There was no help for it. He was going to have to apologize to Rebecca.

Another first for Jake.

* * *

The next morning Rebecca glanced at her watch as she hurried down the stairs. She'd overslept once she'd finally stopped twisting and turning and dropped off. She should probably skip breakfast, but she knew better. She couldn't possibly go to work on an empty stomach. She was going to need all her strength to face the almost certainty of seeing Jake sometime today.

Besides, it would only take an extra ten minutes to—

"Good morning."

The last person she'd expected to find in the sunny breakfast nook was Jake. He was also the last person she'd wanted to see at that particular moment. She hadn't even had the benefit of her first cup of coffee.

"What are you doing here?"

He glanced down at his plate as though it was obvious before he replied. "Having breakfast." He picked up the carafe and poured her a cup of coffee, setting it down at the place across from him. Numbly she sank into the chair, staring at him.

"No, I mean— You're usually at the office by this time."

"I wanted to talk to you, so I waited until your usual time to come down." He glanced at his watch, a tiny frown forming between his eyes.

"I know. I'm late."

He almost smiled. "Somehow I don't think you're going to have to worry about being chewed out by the—"

"Don't say it. I think I've heard enough remarks about—"

"Look, 'Becca, I'm sorry. That's all I was waiting to say. I'm sorry about last night. I'm sorry about my insensitive remarks. I just wish—"

She stared at him in surprise. This was a Jake she'd never seen before. He looked upset. And tired. He wasn't able to cover what he was feeling. "I'm not certain I know what it is you are apologizing for," she said slowly.

"I should never have taken advantage of you."

She raised both brows. "Exactly who took advantage of whom?"

"You know what I mean. I shouldn't have teased you about being the boss."

She tilted her head. "You were teasing?"

His gaze sharpened. "Of course! Besides that, I took advantage of your trust, your having me live here with you. I should never have—"

Rebecca reached for his hand. "Jake, c'mon. You're making this sound as though you plotted and planned to seduce me, when in actual fact, it was I—" Oops, that wasn't exactly what she wanted to admit.

His eyes narrowed. When she didn't say anything more, he prompted, "Yes?"

Hastily she let go of his hand and placed both of hers in her lap. "I guess I just let some of my fantasies overcome my common sense."

Slowly he gave her his very endearing lopsided grin. "Are you saying that you've entertained some fantasies of your own where I'm concerned?"

It was her turn to be surprised. "You've had fantasies about me as well?"

His grin widened. "You'd better believe it."

The knot that had been in her chest suddenly loosened. "Really?"

"You don't need to look so damned pleased about it," he drawled.

"Oh! Well, but it puts everything that happened last night in a whole different perspective."

"All I know is that I never knew how much I'd enjoy making a friend. Look what I've been missing all these years!"

"What?"

He burst out laughing. "Oh, God, 'Becca, but you're so much fun to tease. I'm sorry, but I can't seem to resist trying to provoke you and see that particular look on your face." He pushed back his chair, stood and walked around the table to where she sat. Taking her hand and pulling her up so that she was standing only a few inches away from him, he murmured, "I think we need to begin all over. We should have started this morning's discussion like this." He kissed her, oh so gently, so that if she wished, she could certainly step away. Instead she moved closer, kissing him back. When he finally lifted his head, his eyes were hot.

She felt dazed by the contact, her body already humming with new wants and needs. He stroked her cheek. "Good morning, 'Becca. Did you sleep well last night?"

Rebecca's knees gave way and she sank back down into her chair. How did he do that? She groped for her cup of coffee just as Charles walked into the room carrying her breakfast plate on a tray. She gratefully took the small respite from her overheated emotions to compose herself.

She waited until Charles left the room to murmur, "I slept fine." She gave him a quick glance over her coffee. "And you?"

"Lousy," he replied with a rueful smile. Once again he sat down, this time leaning back into his chair. "A guilty conscience can play hell with your rest, let me tell you."

She looked down at her plate. "I know. I wasn't being completely honest with you, myself. It was after four o'clock before I fell asleep, which is why I overslept this morning."

"About that friendship—"

She decided she needed to eat and took several bites before she realized that he wasn't going to say any more. Looking up at him, she met his intent gaze. "Yes?" she prompted, knowing her heated face was signaling her reaction to his provocative words.

His tone was serious and he didn't smile. "I would never want to lose your regard, 'Becca. You are very special to me. I want you to know that."

She swallowed, her emotions welling up within her. "That's why I was upset last night. Everything that happened was so—was so—" She couldn't find the words to describe her reaction to their making love. "It hurt to hear that you thought I expected you to perform as an employee."

"I didn't mean it. I promise. If you'll recall, you were acting pretty blasé yourself, as though what happened was no more than a carnival ride to be brushed aside once it was over."

She looked down at her plate, then pushed it away. She couldn't think about food right now. "That was my inexperience showing, I'm afraid. I didn't know what I was supposed to do or say."

He picked up her hand and brought it to his lips, kissing her fingertips. "I really am sorry. How can I make it up to you?"

She eyed him for a long moment, seeing that he was truly offering to make amends. Her thoughts flitted back to the night before and all the indescribable sensations she'd experienced.

They could start all over. They could be friends... and more. She knew she was making a decision she might regret later, but she couldn't resist his tempting offer. She withdrew her hand from his with a smile and watched as he reached for his cup.

"Come home earlier tonight and let me indulge in a few more of my fantasies. We might even try a few of yours, as well."

She watched with no small sense of satisfaction as he hurriedly replaced his cup in the saucer before he dropped it. Whatever he might have expected her to say at that point in their conversation, that wasn't it.

"Are you serious?" he asked in a gruff voice, his eyes filled with emotion.

She smiled, unable to speak, but somehow she knew he got his answer.

Seven

Jake thought he had found what he'd been looking for in a file that had been retired several months before. The file contained interoffice memos and reports from the engineering department, of which Troy Wrightman was the head. There wasn't anything concrete, the man was too wily for that, but he'd found the approval for additional expenditures.

What had been going on back then in his department that would have created this flurry of paperwork to cover his activities? Jake leaned back in his chair and rested his head against the back of the chair and came eye to eye with Rebecca, who was leaning against his closed office door across the room.

He blinked and looked around him. It was already

dark outside. He almost groaned out loud. How late was it? He glanced at his watch. After seven.

"How long have you been here?"

She smiled, straightened and sauntered across the room toward him. "It doesn't matter. I saw that you were engrossed in whatever you were reading, and I didn't want to disturb you." She came around the desk. "No, don't get up. I've often thought about what you might do if I were ever bold enough to do this—" She leaned over him, rested her hands on the arms of his chair and kissed him.

He reached for her, tugging her into his lap and wrapping his arms around her.

He'd had trouble concentrating on work all day because he was having a colossal argument with himself. Last night should never have happened . . . last night was the most astounding experience he'd ever had. He would only end up hurting her if he continued what they'd started . . . she was a grown woman and capable of making up her own mind about what she wanted.

She'd made it clear she wanted him almost as badly as he wanted her. How could he argue with something so vital as that?

His heart was thundering in his chest like a herd of wild horses racing by. She felt so good, tasted so good, smelled like a bouquet of flowers. He was starved for her.

She was draped over his lap, her legs resting across the arm of his chair. She was wearing one of her suits with a slim, short skirt. It felt very natural to slide his hand beneath her skirt and between her thighs, feeling the silky smoothness of her hose and discovering they were held up by a lacy garter belt.

He nibbled on her lips and nudged them apart, meeting the tip of her tongue with his. He tensed when he realized that his hand had touched her thick curls and that she was warm and ready for him. She wore no panties.

Jake pulled away from her slightly, only now realizing that she had loosened his tie and unbuttoned his shirt. He slipped his finger into her moistness. "Did you come to work dressed like this?"

She ran her hand across his hair-roughened chest and made what sounded like a sensuous purr deep in her throat. "Of course not. I only took them off before I came in here."

For the first time since he'd looked up and noticed her, he glanced over at the door, wondering who else was still in the building.

She must have read his thoughts. "I locked the door when I came in." She lifted her hips against his hand and kissed him again.

Since he'd spent the day in a half-aroused state, what they were now doing had brought him to full attention.

"Uh...'Becca?"

She was touching his nipple with the tip of her tongue, causing him to shiver. "Mmm?"

"I'm not sure we're going to make it home before—"

"I certainly hope not," she murmured, reaching for his zipper.

They barely made it to the couch before he had her flat on her back and was inside of her. She was so hot and so tight; her enthusiasm was contagious. He couldn't hold back, his strokes coming faster and faster as she wrapped her legs around him.

He felt himself explode when she clamped around him so tightly, her inner contractions draining him until he wasn't certain he'd ever be able to move again.

He collapsed beside her, shifting her slightly so that his weight wasn't completely on her. He lay there, his head resting against her bared breasts and realized that they had managed to discard their jackets and his tie, but otherwise they were still dressed. What clothing remained was thoroughly disarranged, with his pants somewhere around his ankles, her blouse open and her skirt around her waist.

Both continued to wear their shoes.

When he regained some air, he began to laugh.

"What's so funny?" she managed to ask, still panting from their exertions.

"If the board of directors could only see their CEO and president now."

She continued to massage his back and shoulders in a soothing, relaxing stroke. "It's always a good thing to see upper management in accord with one another."

He attempted to push himself up but discovered the muscles in his arms had turned to mush. "I suppose we need to get up sometime."

She sighed contentedly and stretched. "I was thinking about how good the hot tub is going to feel when we get home."

"Hot tub?"

"Mmm-hmm."

After another couple of attempts he managed to sit up. She looked boneless lying there beside him, a very satisfied smile on her face.

"I had lunch with Amanda and Millicent today," she offered in the way of conversation.

"Did you?" he replied, wondering where this was leading.

"Mmm-hmm. They told me to be sure to give you their fondest regards. They asked when I intended to bring you around to the club."

He cupped one of her breasts, stroking the peak until it became rigid. "And what did you say?"

She grinned. "That I wasn't ready to share you just yet."

"So you wanted them to think that—"

"Absolutely. They've been patronizing me for years because I spent most of my time concentrating on my profession rather than my social life. Somehow I believe I owe them a debt of gratitude for the behavior you exhibited that night at the charity ball."

"Well, I did happen to hear bits and pieces of some of their conversation earlier...."

"And decided to show them that they didn't know what they were talking about?"

He leaned down and tugged her hardened peak into his mouth for a few satisfying moments before he admitted, "Something like that."

"Then I owe them my eternal thanks," she said with a sigh, running her fingers through his hair.

Now that the first urgency was gone, Jake knew they should straighten their clothing and go home. But he was finding that he was enjoying the isolation of being high over Seattle and its sparkling lights in the privacy of his office, with only the desk lamp for illumination.

Rebecca appeared content as he continued to smooth his hands along the exposed portions of her body. When she reached for him, stroking him into instant hardness, he discarded the notion of returning home immediately.

Instead he slipped off his shoes, removed his pants and returned his attention exclusively to her.

She was ready for him, her arms sliding around his shoulders as he eased himself back into her warm and waiting depths.

"You're fulfilling another of my fantasies, you know," she whispered into his ear, "making love to me at the office."

He smiled. "Mine, too."

The rest of their communication was without words.

When they finally reached home, their dinner was carefully put away in the refrigerator for them.

"I wonder if the cook gets tired of preparing meals that no one is here to eat," he asked, sitting across the small kitchen table from her, enjoying the contents of the full plate in front of him.

"I asked her that once, several years ago. She said the satisfaction came in knowing that she was preparing tasty, nutritious food. Both Dad and I have always been appreciative of her efforts and often told her so. That seemed to be enough."

"It's been lonely for you, living here since Brock died, hasn't it?"

She glanced around the kitchen. "I've generally kept myself too busy to allow myself to think about it. Of course now that you've been here I've had some time to do other things." She paused and looked at him for a moment before adding, "Would you like to see what I do in my spare time?"

She wore an expression on her face he'd never seen before and it made him very curious. "Of course, if you want to show me."

"I've never told another person, not even my parents. But in the spirit of our new friendship, I believe I'd like you to know."

"You've never told anyone?"

"That's right."

"And you want to tell me?" He found the thought unnerving. No one had ever trusted him with a secret in his entire life.

She smiled. "Yes, I'm rather surprised myself."

As soon as they finished eating, she rinsed their dishes and placed them in the dishwasher. Taking his hand, she led him up the stairs and down the wing to her room.

He'd never seen this part of the house and when he walked into her room, he wondered how she could leave it each day. Although feminine enough, it was the comfort that drew him. There were walls of bookshelves that were crammed with books, a large reclining chair was waiting for her to curl up in for reading, and the soft colors of the room were soothing and relaxing.

"This way." She led him through the bedroom and into a smaller area with lots of floor space and very little furniture. She walked over to a large wall storage unit and unlocked the door. He realized she was pulling out painted canvases and began to smile.

"You paint?"

"Uh-huh." She began to arrange the canvases around the room, facing him. When he saw the subject matter he was drawn to study them up close. She had created an entire underwater world. Soft greens, teals, blues, pinks and rose revealed mermaids and castles, dolphins and sea horses, gleaming crystals, octopuses with wreaths of flowers circling their crowns, schools of brilliantly colored fish.

What an imagination. He glanced at the woman watching him with a tiny smile on her lips. "You did all of these?"

"Yes."

"And you've never shown them to anyone?"

"No. They were my fantasies. There was no reason to share them. Until now."

Once again he had to adjust his perspective of who Rebecca Adams was. He couldn't quite do it. He'd seen her calm, businesslike approach to company situations, he'd seen her handle herself well in social situations, but where had this whimsical person been hiding all of this time?

"I feel honored that you are willing to share these with me."

"That's what friendship is all about, to me."

He turned to her and folded her in his arms. "Thank you for sharing."

She hugged him back. "Thank you for being my friend."

Even though he hadn't meant anything sexual with his hug, holding her pressed against him this way had its usual effect on him.

Without saying anything she stepped back from him, took him by the hand and led him back to her bed.

It was still dark when he awakened, realizing he wasn't alone. Then he remembered. He'd fallen asleep in Rebecca's bed. He couldn't remember the last time he'd slept with someone. He wasn't certain he ever had.

She was sound asleep, her face buried in the pillow, her silky hair flowing over her shoulders. The sheet rested around her waist, revealing the gentle curve of her back.

Jake's heart began to race as fear suddenly took over. For the past several hours he'd lived in the moment, enjoying each new experience without questioning. As 'Becca had once pointed out, he'd forgotten to be the businessman, analyzing everything.

Now, during the small hours of the morning he had to look at what was happening. She spoke of friendship, but wouldn't she want more, expect more? He knew her too well to think she had made the decision lightly to make love with him. He must mean something to her.

The thought scared the hell out of him. He was already too vulnerable where this lady was concerned.

Quietly, so as not to awaken her, Jake eased out of bed and pulled on his pants. After gathering the rest of his clothes together, he slipped out of the room and returned to the other wing and his waiting bed.

His life seemed to be slipping out of his control, especially where his feelings were concerned. He was way over his head in an area he'd always determined he would never explore.

It was time to make some plans for damage control.

Rebecca rolled over onto her back with a sigh and a need to stretch. She felt wonderful, although there was a slight ache where—

She opened her eyes, suddenly remembering why she was experiencing some unaccustomed aches. Jake! She glanced around the room. She was alone. None of his clothes were there.

Looking at the clock, she understood why. It was after seven, past time to be getting ready for work. If she hurried perhaps they could breakfast together, maybe ride to the office together.

With a sensuous smile on her face, she headed to the bathroom for her morning shower, already considering what fantasy she would like to act out next.

When she reached the breakfast room later, she was disappointed to find it empty. "Good morning, Charles," she said, when he brought her morning coffee and toast. "Has Jake already gone?"

"Yes. At his usual time, I believe."

She nodded and took an active interest in the morning paper in order to disguise her disappointment.

Once at the office she had several things to deal with that were waiting on her arrival. It was after eleven before she had an opportunity to ring Jake's office.

"Is Jake in?" she asked Teresa, his secretary.

"He's in conference with Mr. Wrightman. He asked that I hold all of his calls. However, if you—"

"No, no. It's nothing important. Do you know if he has plans for lunch?"

"He didn't say. He generally skips lunch unless I bring something in to him."

"Ah, well. Ask him to give me a call when he's available, will you?"

"Certainly."

Rebecca forced herself to concentrate on what needed to be done for the rest of the day.

Jake had been waiting for Wrightman's call and wasn't surprised when the man called and requested a meeting. Jake was leaning back in his chair, his hands clasped across his middle, when Wrightman arrived.

Troy Wrightman had always reminded Jake of a human-sized praying mantis: tall, thin and a little stoop-shouldered. At the meetings of the department heads he projected an abstracted air, as though running formulas in his head, and rarely speaking.

This morning he looked a little more distracted than usual, but certainly within the realms of normalcy. He didn't suspect a thing.

Jake nodded to one of the chairs. "Have a seat, Troy. How can I help you?"

"I know you explained when you first got here that you would be making changes in the policies and procedures of the company...." He paused, smoothing the sparse hair on top of his head.

Jake waited for him to continue.

"I, uh, understand the concerns you have, and I'm not questioning the necessity of some of the changes." He seemed to run out of steam.

"Glad to hear you're behind me, Troy. You must know how much it benefits a company to have everyone working toward the common good."

"Yes, but— What I mean is— The plant foreman contacted me this morning, explaining that one of our department's designs has been tabled, despite the approval of our customer and the green light from the board." He adjusted his glasses by pushing them up on the bridge of his nose with his forefinger. "He said the order came through last Friday. I was wondering why nobody bothered to tell me, since I'm in charge of development and testing."

Jake continued to lean back in his chair, watching the other man. Instead of answering the question, he asked one of his own. "How long have you been with CPI, Troy?"

Wrightman removed his glasses, shook out a neatly folded white handkerchief and carefully cleaned them. "Fifteen years."

"How long have you been the head of the Engineering Department?"

"Five years next month."

"Do you recall what happened the last time we rushed a newly developed piece of equipment into production?"

Wrightman blinked myopically at him before replacing the glasses. "I'm afraid I don't follow you."

"When did you first decide to deliberately create defects in our new equipment, do you recall?" he asked in a quiet voice.

Wrightman stiffened. "I don't know what you're talking about."

"No. I'm sure you don't. You've really been very clever, playing on the fact that both Brock and the government would want to push all the time restraints in order to get our product out there working." He got up from his chair and said, "Let me walk you back to your office, Troy."

Obviously bewildered, Wrightman stood and followed Jake as he walked out of the office and down the hallway. Jake stepped aside and ushered Wrightman in ahead of him.

Two men were already in the office. One of them was emptying out the drawers into a large box.

Wrightman started toward the desk. "What do you think you're doing in here?" He glanced around at the other man, then at Jake. "Where's Security? Nobody's allowed to come in just like—"

"Let me introduce these gentlemen. They're Federal agents who've been working with me in the investigation of some of the accidents in the plants and the failures of various equipment that was sent out to the government as satisfactorily tested. They're going to escort you and your personal belongings out of the building, then take you down to their office for a chat. I'm sure they'll be able to answer all your questions for you.''

Jake turned and left, striding back to his own office as he checked his watch. His meeting with Wrightman had taken longer than he'd expected. Now he had calls to make, meetings to set up and people to notify. It was going to be another long day, but it was the culmination of all the planning and work he'd done since he'd arrived back in Seattle.

He'd found the man responsible for the problems CPI had been having. What had surprised him was that the man had started long before Brock had died, even before Jake had left. There was enough evidence to nail him, but none of that was his concern. He'd officially turned all of it over to the government when he'd brought Wrightman to the two government agents.

Another week of long days and he should be ready to turn everything back to Rebecca and get the hell out of there. His release from the present situation couldn't come too soon for him.

Eight

Jake made his way through the El Paso International Airport, knowing that Mel would be waiting for him outside the baggage pickup area. He'd called him the day before to see if he'd meet him. It was too far for a cab to take him all the way to Dry Gulch.

As soon as he stepped outside he knew he was back in Texas. Despite the calendar showing it was only mid-May, summer was here. The hot, dry air felt like a sauna after the moist, cloudy weather of the Northwest.

He was glad to be home.

A horn honked nearby and he spotted Mel driving his pickup. It was good to see them both. He grabbed his bags and strode across to where Mel was double parked, tossed the bags in the back of the truck and crawled into the passenger side of the truck's cab.

"Well, don't you look all citified these days," Mel said with a big grin. "Don't guess I ever saw you in a suit before." He pulled into the stream of traffic and headed out of town.

"I left the house early this morning. I had three meetings scheduled before I had to catch the plane. I didn't take time to change clothes."

"Looks like you lost most of your hair while ya were gone."

Jake grinned, running his hand through his carefully trimmed hair. "It'll grow back fast enough, don't worry."

"So where's that li'l gal of yours? I expected to see her with you."

Jake frowned. "Who in the hell are you talking about?"

"That Rebecca that come to fetch you back to Washington with her. When is she going to get here?"

Jake just shook his head. "You get some of the craziest ideas in your head, ol' man. Sometimes I really worry about you. Rebecca hired me to come to work for her temporarily to do a specific job. I did it. Now I've come back home."

"Uh-huh."

"There's nothing between us. Nothing at all."

"'Cept that you been livin' with her for the past four months or so, I understand."

Jake closed his eyes and slowly counted to ten. "Her place is bigger than most hotels, Mel. I rarely saw her."

"Uh-huh."

"So how's Betty?"

"Same as always. How long you fixin' to stay this time?"

"I'm home for good. I did what I set out to do. Now I'm home again."

"Alone."

"Of course I'm alone."

"Humph."

"Crazy ol' coot," Jake muttered under his breath.

"I heard that."

"Good."

"So what you're tellin' me is, there ain't nothin' at all between you and that good-lookin' li'l gal from Seattle."

"That's what I'm tellin' you."

"Then I sure as hell ain't the one sittin' in this here truck that's crazy, that's for certain."

"Could we drop the subject?"

"Consider it dropped."

Jake had already taken his tie off and unbuttoned the top two buttons of his shirt before the plane had left Sea-Tac airport. Now he removed his suit jacket and folded it, placing it on the wide seat between them.

"Park rangers been lookin' for you."

"What do they want?"

"Didn't say."

"What did you tell 'em?"

"That I hadn't seen you in months."

Jake grinned. "That's a fact."

"I'm thinkin' maybe they was afraid you'd done busted your head open clambering around up in them mountains and was lying somewhere up there daid." He looked around at Jake. "'Course I could have reassured 'em by 'splaining that you're too blamed hardheaded to hurt yourself, even if you had hit your head on something."

"I believe you've made your point, Mel."

Mel smiled and refrained from making any more comments for the rest of the trip back to the café.

As soon as they arrived, Betty came rushing to the front door, meeting him as he first stepped inside. She threw her arms around him and hugged him tightly. "Oh, but it's good to see you! I can't believe how much I miss you when I know you ain't tucked up there in them mountains." As soon as she released him, she looked around him, first at Mel, then through the screen door. "You alone?"

Dear God, not her, too! What had gotten into these people, anyway?

"Yes, I'm alone, Betty. No, Rebecca didn't come with me. No, she isn't going to be coming. That's because I didn't ask her, and even if I had, she wouldn't have come. She has a business to run."

She stepped back from him, grabbing her heart. "My goodness, what brought all that on? I jest asked a simple question."

He shook his head and turned away. "I'm going to change clothes. I guess I still have some things in the bedroom, don't I?"

"'Course. By the time you get back, I'll have you a plate of meat loaf and mashed potatoes waiting."

"You always know how to tempt me, don't you, woman?"

She giggled. "Go on now, and get out of them fancy clothes."

Jake went out the back door of the café and followed the path to the place where Mel and Betty had lived as long as he could remember. The house was small but well kept and filled with love. He remembered feeling safe here as a child. Safe and secure.

Now he went into the spare bedroom and peeled out of his clothes. After taking time for a quick shower, he found a frayed pair of jeans to put on, a chambray shirt and the boots he'd left here before he flew to Seattle with Rebecca.

Rebecca.

Funny the way she'd sorta moved into his mind, sneaky like, and taken up residence. Was Mel some kind of a mind reader? How could he possibly have known that Jake had spent most of the flight to Texas reliving the past few days, especially the hours he'd spent with 'Becca?

Of course they'd had to celebrate the arrest of Troy Wrightman, even though she'd felt sorry that his daughter was going to have to suffer through the scandal. All Jake could think about was the fact that Amanda—or was his daughter Millicent?—was going to find out how it felt to be the topic of pitying conversation.

Nothing like instant karma to help learn some of life's little lessons.

The cook had outdone herself that night. Rebecca must have alerted her that they would be home early for dinner. They'd opened a bottle of champagne, eaten, then had talked about what had happened that day and his suggestions regarding what she could do to set up obstacles to deter anyone else attempting such a thing.

Sometime later Rebecca asked, "How about a swim?"

"Sounds good."

She stood and held out her hand. "The staff's all gone upstairs. Let's forget about our suits, okay?"

Instead of taking her hand, he scooped her up in his arms. "There wasn't enough of that suit you were wearing the other night to be considered a swimsuit. Where in the world did you find such a thing?"

"France."

"Figures."

"You didn't like it?"

"What wasn't to like?"

They entered the glass-walled room. The only illumination came from the pool lights. He let go of her and allowed her to slide very slowly down him until her feet touched the floor.

She grinned up at him. "I would say that you're definitely ready...uh, for swimming."

"That, too." He helped her off with her clothes, particularly enjoying removing her high-heeled shoes and carefully rolling down her stockings. Her lacy panties matched her equally lacy, see-through bra. Once she was unclothed, he stepped back to admire his handiwork.

"I wonder if you got the same look on your face when you were unwrapping birthday and Christmas gifts?" she asked with a pleased chuckle.

"I wouldn't be surprised."

He quickly undressed and walked over to the pool before he forgot about swimming and did what he was tempted to do.

"Look. It's raining."

He glanced up at the glassed roof. "So what else is new?"

"It was only misting when we got home."

He dived off the deep end of the pool. When he came up he found that she'd quickly followed him into the water.

"Oh, this feels wonderful," she sighed, floating beside him.

He cupped one of her breasts. "It certainly does."

"Does the rain bother you?"

He slid his arms around her so that he could place his mouth where his hand had been. She arched her back so that her lower body floated against him. Oh, yes. He knew he was definitely ready.

"The rain," she repeated when he brought his head up to kiss her on the mouth. "You don't like it, do you?"

He paused in his endeavors. "Not really. I was raised in the sun. I get tired of the gloom."

"Is that why you live in West Texas?"

"It's my home," he said simply, before searching out her mouth with his. By the time the kiss ended she was clinging to him and he was rapidly losing control. Again.

He nudged her legs around him, bringing her up so that her breasts were at the level of his mouth. He stroked each of them with his tongue, nibbled and tasted until she was squirming against him. With infinite care he lowered her onto him until he was fully encased within her.

"This feels so good," she whispered. "I love to have you so close to me."

He loved it, too. Every time he made love to her, he hoped that this time he would be satisfied. He could no longer blame his response to her on the lack of a woman in his life. Not after these past few weeks. This had to do with this one particular woman.

He would never have known what making love to someone he really loved was like if he hadn't come back to Seattle with Rebecca. He wouldn't have known—

Betty's big white Persian cat leapt up on the bed beside him, bringing him back to the present as he nudged Jake's hand to be petted.

He'd made the right decision, the only decision he could live with. He'd returned to Texas.

Rebecca hadn't acted as though she'd expected him to do anything different. Her cheerful demeanor had made it both easier and more difficult for him to leave.

Didn't she care at all that he was just walking out of her life? Never by word or tone had she indicated that she'd wanted him to stay, that she loved him, or that she might miss him.

He hadn't been forced into making any explanations about his behavior or his feelings. She had accepted everything he'd done and said.

When he'd turned down her offer to take him to the airport, explaining that he would go by cab, she had merely smiled and said, "Well, have a safe flight home. Let us hear from you once in a while."

Of course the other department heads were all there, since the meeting was just breaking up. He and Rebecca weren't given a chance to say goodbye in private, which was just as well.

They'd spent the night before in each other's arms, his silent intensity probably saying more than anything he could have uttered.

So it was over. And he was safely home. Ready to retreat into the mountains once more. This was the life he'd chosen, the life he wanted. Nothing had changed.

"Gotta go, Nuisance," he said to the cat that Mel had named. "I'm looking forward to some of that meat loaf."

The hot July sun beat down on the hidden little valley. The cabin stayed cool enough, nestled within the cave, but Jake found himself staying outside most of the time these days. He was too restless to remain in the cabin long.

At first he'd thought it was because he'd been working so many long hours and that being there in the mountains again was an adjustment. He just needed to learn to slow down and relax a little.

So why hadn't he relaxed?

He'd started dressing for summer now, or more accurately *un*dressing, wearing nothing more than knee-high moccasins and a breechclout. He probably looked more like his mother's people now. This was his usual summer garb. His mother had taught him how to dress as she'd shared some of her history and the history of her people with him when he was a child.

Despite his education and his own belief that he was no different from the other students, he'd been treated differently by everyone. Everyone except Rebecca.

Now that he recalled their conversation when he'd told her about his mother, he realized that she'd never pursued the information she'd elicited from him. She'd never once referred to it again. She'd accepted it as she'd accepted everything about him.

How could he help loving her?

What he hadn't been prepared for was how much he missed her. He'd thought the loss would lessen, that the ache would go away. He'd treated her like an addiction he'd intended to kick.

But he had no control over his dreams, nor over the number of times he thought about her during the day. Wasn't there a country song that mentioned something about thinking of a person only twice a day— once all night and once all day? He seemed to be coming close to that.

There wasn't anything to be done about her. Their worlds were more than miles apart. He could function in both worlds, but he realized after spending those four months at the company that the challenge was gone. He'd enjoyed searching out a specific problem, but the everyday running of the operations was tedious.

He thought he'd been so damned high-minded about walking away last year. He was beginning to see his behavior from a different perspective. The truth was that he hadn't wanted to face the fact that he'd pursued that life-style to prove that he could, that he was as good as anyone. He'd shown his absent father, he'd shown Brock, his substitute father, and he'd proven it to himself.

Despite all the luxury that had surrounded him, he'd yearned for the wide open spaces. Maybe there was more of his mother's blood in him than he'd ever wanted to acknowledge.

So he should be content now. He had everything he wanted.

Except Rebecca.

Glancing around the meadow, he couldn't remember how many times he'd wished she were there to see how lush and green it had become now that everything was in bloom and the deciduous trees had leafed out.

The deer herd seemed to be increasing and he'd wanted her to see the fawns.

He'd taken to sleeping outside at night where he'd lay for hours looking up at the stars, wondering if she could even see them with the habitual cloud cover of her area.

With a grunt of frustration, Jake made up his mind to work off some of his restlessness. He'd go hiking through the mountains, check out the different areas.

Hell, he might even look up a park ranger or two.

One more night, in a string of sleepless nights, Rebecca lay in bed staring up at the ceiling, wondering what Jake was doing these days. Did he ever think of her? Somehow she doubted it.

She wished she could stop thinking about him. No matter how busy she was at the office, her mind always seemed to return to him.

She'd implemented his suggestions, promoted one of the department heads to president and did everything possible to avoid going to his office. She had too many memories of the place.

She'd gotten into the habit of swimming each evening in the futile hope that she would tire herself out enough to fall asleep instead of lying there night after night missing Jake.

She'd been downright proud of herself the day he'd left. She hadn't cried until after she'd gotten home that night. She hadn't fallen on her knees and begged him to stay, although she might have if she'd thought for a minute he would have listened.

However, he'd made it clear that he was marking off the days until he could return to his beloved hideaway in the mountains.

She rolled over and punched her pillow. Well, good for him. She was glad that at least one of them was happy!

Of course, it wasn't his fault that she'd wanted more than he was prepared to offer. Hadn't she found out enough about his early life to know that he wasn't about to allow anyone to get close to him?

He didn't have any idea what a family life could be. He'd never known his father. How could he possibly be expected to know?

No. She knew he was a loner. She even knew why. He found it safer not to trust anyone. He was just like one of those untamed animals living up there in the mountains.

She smiled to herself. Wouldn't he be something, though, to keep around, if he could be coaxed in from the wilds? Didn't she know more about him than anyone? Just as he knew more about her than anyone? Didn't she stand a better chance of taming him? What if there was one chance—maybe one in a thousand, but still, one chance—of making it work? Didn't she owe it to them both to try?

Her eyes drifted shut as she sleepily wondered about her vacation schedule. She used to spend her vacations in the mountains, didn't she? So maybe this year, just maybe...

She fell asleep thinking about Jake.

Nine

Jake came through the long cave and paused at the opening to his own private paradise. He was tired, but it was a good tired. He'd pushed himself for the past week, hiking for miles, checking out new trails, sleeping out each night. When he finally stopped for the night, he was so tired that he fell into an exhausted sleep.

Somewhere along the way he'd made a certain peace with himself. He'd reminded himself that he'd gotten over the loss of his mother eventually. He still missed having her in his life, but there was no longer the gaping loss he'd felt those first years after her death.

So he knew it was just a matter of time until he got over Rebecca. He had plenty of time. He never had a reason to see her again. She had her own life, more money than she could possibly spend in three life-times. She would probably marry one of these days, somewhere in the future.

There. He'd said it. He would just get used to the idea that she would find her own happiness with someone else.

He started down the narrow, sloping path to the floor of the meadow. The hot Texas sun had him dripping with perspiration. Maybe he'd take a dip in the creek. There was a place just before it disappeared beneath the mountain that had been hollowed out where the water was deep enough to swim.

He took a quick glance around the meadow. Everything looked the same as it did a week ago. At least there was enough water to keep everything looking green. He would be glad to—

Jake paused, staring at the place where he swam. Someone was there, sunning on one of the rocks. He took off in a loping run. Who the hell had managed to find his valley? In all the years he'd lived there nobody had ever been there before. Nobody but—

Rebecca?

She sat up, pushing her hair away from her face before she inched down to the water. She hadn't seen him approaching, but he was now close enough to recognize her and to see that she hadn't bothered to wear anything for her summer dip in his creek.

He watched her slip into the water, then dive below for a few feet before reappearing at the surface. Only then did she spot him as he neared the creek.

"Jake? Goodness, I hope that's you! You look just like an Indian dressed like that." She swam toward him and rose out of the water to meet him for all the world as though she were fully clothed. "You're certainly dark enough," she added, continuing to stare at him uncertainly.

"You better damned well be glad it's me, woman," he growled, jerking off his moccasins by hopping on first one foot, then the other. "You seemed to have misplaced your swimsuit."

Somewhere during his response, she let out a whoop of total and pleased recognition and launched herself at him. If he hadn't braced himself they would have both fallen.

"Oh, I'm so glad to see you!" she said, wrapping herself around his neck. "You look gorgeous with that deep tan! Absolutely gorgeous. Have you ever thought about doing any modeling?"

He didn't touch her. He couldn't touch her. If he laid a finger on her, all the hard work he'd done for the past two months would be wasted. Like an alcoholic who knew better than to take one sip, he knew better than to touch her.

"What are you doing here, Rebecca?" he asked through clenched teeth, his arms at his sides.

One thing he had to say for her, she was always quick to understand a situation.

She stepped back from him, staring into his face. "I came to see you," she replied. "I was hoping you'd be glad to see me."

He gave a quick flick of a glance at her nude body. "Well, you're certainly giving me ample opportunity to see as much as possible."

Only then did she seem to become aware that she wasn't dressed. She spun away and scooped up a large towel, quickly wrapping it around her.

"What's wrong? Are you angry with me?"

He waded into the water without looking at her. "How did you get here?"

She stood beside the creek and watched him as he submerged himself, then came up and shook the water out of his face, skimming his hands over his hair.

"Mel drove me up to where your truck's parked. I hiked in the rest of the way."

"That was a stupid thing to do. You could have gotten lost so badly that nobody would have ever been able to find you."

She sat down on the rock and watched him as he allowed the water to cool him off. "I have a good sense of direction and I had been here before, remember."

"An obvious mistake on my part," he muttered.

He could see the hurt in her face, and he didn't want to cause her pain, damn it. He just wanted her to stay out of his life. Now he was going to have to start all over getting used to not hearing the sound of her voice, not smelling the scent that was distinctively hers—of flowers and sunshine and clean, healthy woman.

"I thought we were friends, Jake," she finally said quietly. "I took some vacation time and thought it would be nice to spend it with you here in the mountains."

"You should have checked with me first."

"How could I? Mel and Betty said you hadn't been down there since you first got home. I'd called them earlier. Unless you have some carrier pigeon form of communication I didn't know how to check with you." She looked away from him, toward the cabin. "As it turned out, you weren't here, anyway. I got here three days ago. Since I told Mel that I'd get you to drive me back down the mountain, I didn't have any choice but to wait until you showed up."

He came out of the water, picked up his backpack and said, "C'mon. It's too hot to stay out here in the sun."

She didn't say anything, just followed him across the meadow to the cabin. Once inside he saw that she had made herself at home. She'd baked some biscuits and there was a stack of canned goods on the counter that she must have brought with her.

"I'm sorry, Jake," she said, standing in the doorway. "I didn't mean to intrude. I just thought—" She gave a tiny wave of her hand. "I don't know, that we could just—"

"We could pick up where we left off, is that it? That we could just hop into the sack for old-time's sake? Is that what you thought?"

She walked over to a knapsack he hadn't noticed earlier and pulled out a pair of shorts and a colored T-shirt. She slipped them on beneath the towel, then used the towel to dry her hair. "Would that be so wrong?" she asked.

That's when he knew he was lost. How could he possibly fight this woman when the mere sight of her was like water to a man lost in the desert. "Oh, 'Becca," was all he could force out of his throat. In two strides he was by her side, hauling her into his arms. "Oh, God, 'Becca."

He buried his face in her hair and clung to her, inhaling her sweetness, hating himself for being so weak, hating himself for needing her so damn much.

"'Becca."

It was only when she lifted her head and looked at him, then tenderly touched his cheek with the tips of her fingers, that he realized his blurred vision was because of the tears in his eyes.

She looked at him in bewilderment. "I thought you didn't want me here," she said slowly.

He just shook his head. He couldn't speak. If he tried to tell her, he would break down completely.

"What's wrong, Jake? Please tell me."

And the words came tumbling out of him from somewhere deep within his soul. "I love you, 'Becca. God have mercy. I love you."

"Oh, Jake," she whispered, her eyes filling as well, while her face glowed. "I didn't know. You never said. Never. I've tried so hard not to love you—"

"Me, too," he managed to say.

"But I can't help it." She buried her head in his chest.

"Me, either." He wrapped his arms around her and held her to him, never wanting to let her go.

He lost track of time as they stood there in the middle of the cabin, clinging to each other. Her words slowly came back to him. She loved him. *Rebecca loved him.* She had come to Texas to see him, to be with him. Because she loved him.

A warmth seemed to fill his chest, as though something had suddenly begun to grow, like a bud blossoming into full flower. She was here now.

And she was his.

It was only a few steps to the bed, and neither one of them were wearing much. With a few efficient moves, even the few scraps were gone and they were loving each other, almost frantic in their need to touch, to kiss, to possess. He was buried deep inside her and she had her arms and legs wrapped tightly around him before they paused for more than a panting breath.

He looked down at her and said, "I don't think I can go on without you in my life."

The smile she gave him was so sweet it made his heart ache with tenderness. "You don't have to, love. You never did."

There were no more words. He tried to show her how he felt with every touch and every move. She couldn't seem to get enough of him, either, and her kisses and caresses sent him over the edge. He let out a cry and surged deeply in one final thrust, clutching her in his arms.

They lay there for a long time without speaking. Jake didn't know what to say. He was at a loss. Everything he ever thought he knew about himself had just disintegrated and drifted away.

"You have an interesting way of greeting visitors to your home, Jake. Confusing, but interesting."

"Do you have any recommendations for improvement?"

She ran her hand along his bare flank and sighed. "Oh, I don't think so, although there are certain elements I wouldn't wish to see repeated with anyone but me."

"I might point out the same thing. What if that hadn't been me who came upon you swimming in the nude, hmm?"

"You'd already told me nobody else knew how to find the place. Although, I must admit when I first spotted you I thought Geronimo had come back to haunt his old stomping grounds!"

He ran his fingers through her damp hair. "That's never bothered you, has it?"

"What?"

"My mixed blood."

"Why should it? I've got all kinds of mixed blood in me...French, Irish, Welsh, English."

"You know what I mean."

"Jake, there's no such thing as a pure blooded anything, don't you know that? Even among native tribes, there's intermingling of bloodlines. And what difference does it make, anyway? Each of us is the very person we're supposed to be, a perfect blend of all our ancestors' hopes and dreams of the future." She stretched her arms up in the air for a moment before returning them to his back where she trailed her hands along his spine. "Why should we want to be anything other than that?"

He sighed and rolled over onto his back, holding her so that she sprawled across him. "When did you get to be so wise?"

She raised her head. "I'm not sure of the exact moment. What time is it?"

He laughed. So did she.

"So what do we do now?" he finally asked.

"Eat?" she asked hopefully.

He sat up, still holding her. "Good idea, but that wasn't quite what I was talking about."

She tilted her head. "You mean you want to get into some heavy discussion about the future?"

"Not particularly, but I think it's called for, about now. Let's face it. Our life-styles couldn't be more different. Somehow we're going to have to figure out a way to live together where we'll both be content."

"That won't be difficult. I'll be content wherever *you* are. And our son will be content wherever *we* are. So it's merely a matter of your deciding what you want and where you—"

He'd stiffened at the unexpected word. "Our son?"

She slipped off his lap and gathered up her clothes, hastily pulling them on. "Mmm, yes. Well, I didn't quite mean to spring him on you in exactly that manner—"

Jake grabbed her by the arm. "Our son?" he repeated. "Are you trying to tell me that you're pregnant?"

"Like I said, until you establish a reliable pigeon service into the valley—"

"Damn it, 'Becca. I'm not joking!"

She paused and looked at him calmly. "Neither am I. That's one of the reasons I'm here. Yes, I did need a vacation, and yes, I do enjoy visiting the mountains, but I also thought you needed to know that you're going to become a father."

He spun away from her and strode to the front door that they'd left open. "I never gave it a thought! Not once! Well, except for a fleeting moment in the hot tub. How could I have been so stupid? So careless? So—"

"Loving?" She touched his arm softly. "I didn't do anything, either, and I could have. To be very honest with you, I was hoping I would become pregnant. I couldn't be more thrilled."

He leaned against the doorframe and stared down at her. "Glad?" he repeated weakly.

"Absolutely. I can't think of better daddy material than you, and I'm going to be a whale of a mommy." She grinned. "Literally, in a few short months."

"When? When is it due?"

"He. It's a he. He's due right after the first of the year. There's a chance he'll be born on the first. Wouldn't that be something? A brand new baby for a brand new year?"

She looked so damned pleased with herself, as though she'd personally pulled off a miracle.

A miracle was right.

"I don't know the first thing about being a father."

"Well, you've done just fine so far."

"We can't stay here, that's for sure. I'll move to Seattle. I'll—"

"Whoa, hoss. We don't have to make all those decisions today. Food is definitely at the top of my list of priorities. Then maybe a nap. You wouldn't believe how sleepy I get these days. My secretary knows to check on me by two each afternoon to make certain I'm awake. I tend to doze after lunch, nap after dinner, but then I perk back up and—"

"Do people know your pregnant?"

"Not yet, but it isn't something you can hide for long."

"Once we're married, we'll tell them we got married before I left. There's no reason to have them gossiping and counting fingers."

"I never concern myself with gossip, and there's no reason for us to get married."

He placed his hand over her abdomen. "Yes, there is."

"Not unless you want to. I didn't come here to suggest a shotgun wedding. We'll still be parents, no matter what."

"I don't want to have to explain to him why we aren't married. I love you. I want you to be my wife."

"Funny you never mentioned it before."

"Rebecca," he drawled warningly.

"In fact, I remember Dad mentioning something about your setting him straight about helping to continue a dynasty."

He looked at her, horrified. "He told you that?"

She grinned. "Yeah. He did. We both thought it was funny."

"You weren't hurt by it?"

"Why should I be? You didn't know me. You weren't interested in getting to know me and to be real honest, I was too uncomfortable around you to even consider spending any more time in your company than I absolutely had to."

"So it was Brock's idea?"

"No more than a passing thought, from what I could tell."

"I still want to marry you."

She was busy opening cans and preparing a meal. "When?" she asked without looking up.

"As soon as possible. Tomorrow. We'll drive into El Paso. I want it done."

"Okay. We'll take Mel and Betty, okay?"

He set the table. "I doubt they'd go. There's no one to watch the café."

"Then they'll close it." She turned and put her arms around his waist. "I can guarantee you that given the chance to see you get married, the Abbots wouldn't miss it for the world."

"It will all work out. I know it will."

She began to laugh. "I have every confidence that it will. You, on the other hand, have all the enthusiasm of a man on the way to the dentist for a root canal."

"That's because I'm scared, 'Becca. I'm way over my head. Before an hour ago I would never have imagined that I would ever get married or become a father."

"Yes, I know, but you had no compunction about making those choices. Don't you see, Jake? That's what life's all about, anyway. It's not about having all the answers. It's about making choices as they come up, one at a time. Then dealing with the next choice. We don't have to make all those choices in one day. It's enough that you're finally back from your mountain walkabout, that I've been able to relay the information of your impending fatherhood, and that you've admitted that you love me. There's some pretty monumental stuff going on here, you know.''

"To think I might have missed all of this," he said, sitting down across from her and watching her avidly fill her plate. Motherhood obviously agreed with her.

He only hoped he could handle the new roles he'd committed himself to. What if he was like his father? What did he know about babies? What—

She reached over and took his hand. "You helped me when I really needed you, when nobody else could help. Now it's my time to help you. Give me a chance, and I'll prove to you that you'll be able to come through all of this like the seasoned pro you are. We'll take it one step at a time, okay?''

"As long as you're a part of my life, I know I can handle whatever comes."

"Count on it, love. I'll always be there."

Epilogue

Betty looked around the café, checking to see if any of their customers needed anything. There was a cheerful din of voices in the room now at lunchtime. Business always picked up in the summer after school was out and families were traveling on vacation.

She glanced out the window as yet another minivan pulled in and parked. She watched as a tall, broad-shouldered, long-legged man got out of the van and walked around to the passenger side. He opened the door for the woman sitting there, slipped some kind of canvas carryall around his neck, then took a sleeping infant from the woman's arms and carefully placed the baby in the baby-toting canvas.

Betty leaned into the window between the dining

area and the kitchen. "They're finally here, Mel," she called, her voice quavering with excitement.

"It's about time!" he hollered back.

Betty was already heading toward the front door when it burst open and a seven-year-old dynamo came racing through it. "Gramma! Granpa! Guess what we did! We saw the Great Canyon place, it's a big hole in the ground and Daddy made me hold his hand and Jennie got scared and she cried and then we saw—"

"You don't have to tell them about our entire trip during the first five minutes we're here, son," came a deep voice behind him. The tall man with the sleeping baby nestled against his chest held the door open for his wife, who was guiding their three-year-old daughter through the door.

Betty was already receiving a bear hug by the time the rest of the family got inside.

She straightened just in time to sweep the little girl up into her arms. "Hi, Jennie. Do you remember me?"

The little girl had her thumb in her mouth. She nodded, but didn't remove the comforting presence to speak. Still holding her, Betty walked over to the man and said, "You look plumb natural with a passel of kids hanging on to you, Jake. Let me get a peek at this little guy you've got there."

Jennie removed her thumb long enough to announce, "That's Joey."

"Well, how about that? Joey, huh? Do you like having a li'l brother?"

Jennie popped her thumb back into her mouth and nodded.

Mel came out of the kitchen and hugged Rebecca. "I swear, woman, you get better lookin' every day. Having kids certainly seems to be agreeing with you."

Rebecca hugged him back. "Oh, Mel, you don't know how much that means to me to hear!"

Jake looked around at her, affronted. "I'm always telling you how good you look, 'Becca. Why's it any different coming from this ol' buzzard?"

"'Cause she knows I'm sincere. Just as she knows that you're always sweet to her 'cause you generally want something from her, ain't that right?" Mel asked Rebecca.

Her cheeks flushed as she looked at her husband, his black-eyed gaze daring her to comment.

Betty motioned to them and started toward an empty booth in the back. "Come on back here and sit. I bet those young 'uns are hungry by now."

"They're always hungry," Jake muttered.

"I've got a high chair for Jennie and a booster chair for Jason, and if you want me to, I can hold Joey for you while you eat."

"He's fine where he is," Jake growled.

Rebecca held out a hand to each of the children. "Let's go wash up, kiddos, so we can eat, okay?"

Jake folded his long length into the back booth, his arm cradling the baby. Mel turned back to the kitchen while Betty arranged the children's chairs.

"So you stopped by the Grand Canyon on your way home this time. I guess the kids really enjoyed it."

Jake rolled his eyes. "I don't know about Jennie, but Jason is already planning his next trip back. He intends to ride one of the mules to the bottom of the canyon.''

Betty paused, beaming, and studied Jake. ''You're looking mighty good these days. Pretty pleased with yourself. It's a wonder that shirt has any buttons left on it.''

''I can't complain. Of course I'm always glad to get back home. Now that Jason's in school we have to plan our summer visits around his schedule.''

''Do you mind it so much, being there in Seattle the rest of the time?''

He grinned. ''Not really. For some strange reason 'Becca seems to feel she has to make it up to me, so she works real hard at making sure I'm not pining away for my mountain home.''

The children came running back into the room just ahead of their mother and clambered into their chairs. Rebecca looked at Jake and grinned. ''Keeping them cooped up in the car all day isn't the smartest thing we could do. They're so wired we're going to need a butterfly net to catch them.''

''They can run it off once we get to the valley.''

Betty spoke up. ''I bet you're glad the forest service people built some more roads up there, so you don't have so far to walk these days.''

''You're telling me,'' Rebecca replied. ''It made building the new house a great deal more simple. All of us couldn't have fitted into that one-room cabin any more.''

Betty said, ''You never did tell me how you managed to get the government to let you lease your land all legallike.''

Jake winked at Rebecca. "Well, I married into a pretty influential family, who know some fairly important people who knew what strings to pull to get me a hearing."

"His charm did the rest," Rebecca added, batting her eyes at him.

"That don't surprise me none," Betty said. "That boy's always been one to go after what he wants without ever givin' up." She glanced around. "Looks like our lunch rush is about over. Let me go take some of these people's money and I'll be back to catch up on all your news. Mel should have your meals about ready."

Rebecca waited until Betty was out of earshot before she murmured, "Do you think those two are ever going to slow down? Retire? Maybe do some traveling?"

"Traveling? No. No way. This place is what keeps 'em young. Things slow down in the winter, but they both enjoy the bustle and noise of the families who come through."

"Are you sure you don't want me to take the baby?"

Jake gave her a mock-ferocious stare. "What's all this push to get Joey away from me? Can't you tell he's doing just fine?"

She grinned. "Well, I have to admit he's found one of my favorite places to curl up and nap." To her delight she actually saw his cheeks redden. "I can't believe it. You're blushing!"

"Am not. I'm just getting a little sun is all."

"Sure. Right here in the café." She laughed. "I want to compliment you on how patient you are being with this stop. I know if you had your way you'd already be racing up the mountain to be sure everything's the way you left it last fall."

"I'm not *that* bad."

"Almost. All you have to do is say the word and we can move over here year-round. We've even got phone service up there now. We can move our computers, our faxes and stay in touch with the plant if you want."

"What about Jason's schooling?"

"It might mean a little commuting, but I wouldn't mind. You've lived in my world for the past eight years without complaining. I can certainly do the same thing for you."

"I didn't have anything to complain about. I'd rather live in Seattle with you, rain and all, than in the mountains alone."

"But what about living in the mountains with all of us?"

He smiled wistfully. "That would be a dream come true."

"See? Your every wish is my command. I've been talking with the other officers in the company about the possibility of phasing us out of the daily operations. We've already learned that I'm not indispensable when I took my maternity leaves."

"You'd do that for me, 'Becca?"

"I'd do anything for you, Jake. Anything at all."

Betty brought a tray with all their lunches. She'd brought the adults the luncheon special, Jake's favorite meat loaf and mashed potatoes, and the children got hamburgers and french fries. Now that the place had cleared out, she dragged up a chair and sat down, plying them with questions.

Part of Jake joined in the conversation while another part detached and looked around him. He was surrounded by the people he loved and who loved him.

No one could ever have convinced him that his life would have taken such a turn. He couldn't possibly have imagined having a wife and children.

Some nights he still sat beside their beds and watched them sleep, still in awe of the miracle that he'd been a part of. He marveled at how tiny and trusting they were, so filled with love and affection for everyone around them.

They'd helped him to deal with his fears by their simple presence in his life.

And 'Becca. Where would he be without her? A part of him must have known that she was to be his future. Why else would he have been so careless about something as important as birth control? Hadn't his own life taught him what could happen with an unwanted pregnancy?

None of these pregnancies had been unwanted. Unexpected, maybe, but each one had been a blessing he'd been afraid he didn't deserve.

As if all of that wasn't enough, 'Becca was willing to consider moving permanently to Texas. Maybe he didn't need it so much now. He'd still have his summers here. Besides, the business needed him. Maybe he needed the business just as much.

Did it really matter where they lived? The important thing was that they had created a family together. Just imagine, they had been two "only" children—both alone—who after finding each other discovered they had so much love to give.

Joey stirred, stretching and yawning, making little noises. Jake kissed him on his fuzzy little head and smiled.

He'd finally discovered what was really important in life.

Jake glanced up and saw Rebecca watching him, her smile so full of love that he struggled with the lump that suddenly filled his throat.

"Well, Papa Jake, are you tired of holding your squirming son yet?" she asked.

"'Fraid not, but since I'm not equipped to feed him, guess I'll have to give him up, anyway, at least for the moment."

Betty and Rebecca laughed, and he was able to hand the baby over and quickly wipe away the moisture in his eye before the women in his life caught him being sentimental.

Mountain men had to keep up a certain image, after all.

* * * * *